A CRUMBY WAY TO DIE

A KC CRUMB MYSTERY

GEORGIANA DANIELS

Cozy Cove Press

To my Chloe Belle, for all the love and fun.

Chapter One

PRO TIP: when life hands you lemons, hand them back and demand coffee. High octane coffee, to be more specific. One had to be hyper-caffeinated to survive what I'd been through since recently moving back to Beaver Bluff.

"He's still out there." Naomi wrinkled her nose as she peered out the window of Crumb's Bakery, where I worked part-time to help my aunt, Lulu Crumb.

Naomi and Polly, my aunt's oldest friends, huddled with me at a table to watch my ex-boyfriend. He paced the sidewalk with his messenger bag slung over his shoulder and his phone pinned to his ear.

A few days ago, James had shown up on my doorstep with flowers and flimsy promises. Worse, he'd interrupted what would have been an epic kiss with Officer Antonio Hamson, who'd quickly vanished into the night. I hadn't seen or heard from Hamson since, while James, on the other hand, kept popping up like a whack-a-mole.

Polly flipped the page of the latest issue of *AARP*. "Is there a reason James won't come inside?"

"Maybe because I told him not to bother me." I took a swig of dark-roast coffee. The morning rush was over, and only a handful of customers lingered inside the bakery, giving me a few moments to regroup. "I thought he'd take the hint and go back to LA."

Polly snorted. "I'm pretty sure a guy with a man bun that size isn't big on taking hints."

I set my mug down with a clatter. "What's his hair have to do with anything?" I touched my hair self-consciously, hair that made me look like a zebra after a recent highlighting incident. At least, according to Polly, who had no filter.

"Just pointing out that there's nothing subtle about that guy, from his hair to his…oh, never mind." Polly shrugged. Her own dyed-brown, pageboy haircut hadn't changed in decades.

"I kind of like his man bun. Gives him a chic, mysterious look. *Va-vroom.*" Naomi waggled her gray eyebrows.

Polly licked her finger and turned another page. "Good luck getting Walter to grow one of those."

Walter was Naomi's new boyfriend, although referring to someone in his seventies as a boyfriend felt odd. But now that Naomi and Walter were together all the time, Polly was feeling a little left out. So I decided to cut her some slack.

"You might be right. James probably needs more than a subtle hint. Maybe I'll talk to him when my shift is over." I glanced at the cat clock on the wall. It was almost time for the afternoon crew to take over for the last few hours and help my Aunt Lulu prep for tomorrow.

I opened the notes app on my phone and started to make plans. As soon as I got rid of James, I'd head downtown to meet with my newest client, a struggling jewelry store manager. Now that I was using my social media marketing skills as a freelancer for local businesses, I kept a full schedule.

"I'd better get back at it. Looks like Krystal needs help." I glanced at the short line forming at the counter.

"I need to leave, too." Naomi stood and grabbed her coat off the back of her chair. "I'm meeting Walter at his ice cream shop before his afternoon rush." Her cheeks reddened as she smiled and waved goodbye.

Just then, Aunt Lulu ambled over with a man I'd never seen before. She flung her gray braid over her shoulder. "KC, there's someone I'd like you to meet."

"Hi, how are you?" I offered my hand to a middle-aged man with a bristly brown mustache that hung so far over his top lip I thought he'd bite it when he spoke.

"Fine. My name's Mason Dunn." He looked back at Lulu. "Really, I don't think I need the whole social media thing. I'm kicking around the idea of selling the business and moving on."

"Nonsense." She waved him off. "KC does more than just social media. She does marketing and promotions and special events, too."

"I'd like to see you fit that on a business card," Polly chuckled.

"Oh, Polly." Lulu playfully whapped her friend's shoulder. "Don't listen to her," she said to Mason. "KC is the best there is when it comes to increasing your business's profile." Aunt Lulu ushered us to an empty table by the window, seemingly unaware of James pacing just outside or of Mason's resistance to working with me.

"I don't know what a profile is or if I even need one," Mason said.

Aunt Lulu ignored Mason's protests. "You two chat for a few minutes while you wait for your sister." She turned to me. "He and his sister are the owners of the Beaver Bluff Bed and Break-fast, and they're getting ready for a big event." She winked at me before she strolled back to the counter to help with the next few people in line.

"That's interesting." I gestured for Mason to take the seat across from me as I sat down and studied him. Average build with drab khaki clothing that would blend into any surroundings. The only thing notable about him was the walrus mustache. I smiled. "Tell me about your B&B."

"We've been around a little less than a year, and we're doing okay. That's why I don't think we need whatever it is you're offering." He started to rise, and I was half-tempted to let him walk away. But alas, I needed more clients.

I motioned for him to stay seated. "No pressure here. You're welcome to hang out while you wait for your sister." Maybe I'd have better luck with her. "What's her name?"

He grimaced. "Dana. The B&B is mostly her thing."

"Then what's your thing?" I asked, genuinely interested.

"I handle the business side. Probably not something you know a whole lot about."

I narrowed my eyes. "Let's not make assumptions."

"I meant the B&B business." Mason's tone was unapologetic. "Your aunt seems to think I should ask your advice about a get-together we're hosting tomorrow night."

"Tell me about it." I plowed ahead, determined not to let his brusque manner get the better of me in front of James, who glanced through the window every few moments.

"We're hosting a local law firm. They're celebrating their tenth anniversary." Mason's mustache twitched. "I think I've got it handled."

I raised my eyebrow at him.

"Plus, it seems rude to ask at the last minute."

That was the least rude thing he could do at this point. I considered my already crowded schedule. If I skipped my work-out, I could make time for the B&B. "I can look at what you already have planned and see if you're missing anything. It never hurts to have an extra pair of eyes. I have checklists that might help." Or I would as soon as I had a moment to type one up. I mentally kicked myself for the half-truth, something that never bothered me until I moved back to Beaver Bluff and started hanging out with my new bestie, Verity, who insisted on sharing the absolute truth at all times.

Mason's face relaxed a fraction as though he were considering my offer.

A gust of wind blew in as James opened the door and headed

toward me. Polly lifted the magazine to cover the lower half of her face, her eyes laser-focused on us.

Heat flooded my veins at my ex's nearness. I needed him to be gone, as far from Beaver Bluff as possible. My life had finally taken a turn for the better, and here he was, ready to mess it all up again. I fought to hold back a torrent of angry words. There were so many things I'd wanted to say when I left LA after catching him with another woman. Then he fired me from my position as the social media manager for Swanky Shoes and More.

"Can we talk?" James's gaze intensified as he spoke. "Please?"

"I'm with a client." I sat taller and motioned to Mason.

He shook his head. "I'm not actually a client."

"See?" James said.

I looked between Mason and James. "But he will be," I said through clenched teeth.

"I think you need to talk to my sister." Mason held up his hands in a surrender position. "The whole party stuff is more of a lady thing."

"You can talk to his sister," James echoed.

Polly scowled, and I motioned for her to stay back. While I wasn't a fan of Mason either, Polly was the one more likely to clock him for his "lady thing" comment. She snapped the magazine back open and angrily flipped a page.

"It's just that…." James's voice broke, and he took a moment to compose himself. "I may have to leave today."

"Don't let the door hit you," Polly said.

James glanced at her, confused. Then he turned back to me. "This may be the last chance I have to make things right with you."

"After what you did, there's no making things right." I practically spat the words before remembering I was with a potential client, albeit one I had mixed feelings about. "In any case, have a pleasant drive. Say hi to Crissy for me." Even the name of the woman who'd replaced me—both personally and professionally—soured on my tongue.

"But you don't…it's not like that with Crissy." James's forehead wrinkled as he pleaded with me. "If you would just listen, I could explain. I don't have much time because there aren't any more available hotel rooms."

"I have a room," Mason piped in.

Polly and I groaned in unison.

"Really?" James perked. "I thought I tried everything."

"I own the Beaver Bluff Bed and Breakfast downtown. We had a cancelation this morning. It was for a week-long stay."

James threw off a million-dollar smile. "Dude, that's rad. Thanks, I'll take the whole week."

Polly and I both face-palmed ourselves. The fact that I was twinning with Polly should have worried me, but I was more concerned about how I would get rid of my ex.

"Your little lady here seems to think she can help me with my B&B." Mason jerked his chin toward me.

I tensed. "Hey, now. Don't call me—"

"She's the best in the business." James held his hand out, as if to keep me from launching across the table. "Tell you what, if you don't see a return on your investment, I'll cover her fee myself."

My fee just doubled. Not that I wanted to work with Mason anymore, but at the same time, I didn't want to look like a failure in front of James while he was trying to play knight in shining armor. What a mess.

Mason stroked his mustache. "Sounds like an offer I can't refuse. You can head over and check-in whenever you're ready."

"I'll be there as soon as I finish talking to KC." James's gaze softened when he turned to me.

"KC, you can come by and talk party stuff with my sister whenever you want." Mason glanced around. "Looks like she's not going to make it here today."

"A party?" James glanced between us.

"It's tomorrow night. You can join us since you'll be there, anyway." Mason stood, then pushed in his chair and shook hands with James. Then the blowhard left.

My blood pressure dialed down a few ticks. "I can't believe what just happened."

"You can thank me later." James grinned. "Or now. We should talk."

"I'm super busy." I rose and dusted my hands.

"There's no use trying to avoid me. Even if we don't talk now, I'll still see you at the party tomorrow night."

"Not if I see you first."

James chuckled as though he didn't believe me. "Don't worry, I can wait until tomorrow. We'll hang out and catch up. It'll be cool."

Another gust blew through the door as Antonio Hamson strolled into Crumb's with an air of cool confidence. He wore jeans and a Henley that stretched taut over his broad chest, his casual outfit indicating he was off duty. His dark eyes scanned the room and landed on...us.

James smirked when he caught Hamson's gaze. Then he turned to me and raised his voice. "Great, then it's a date." He bumped Hamson with his messenger bag on his way to the door.

"It's not a date!" I called after him, ignoring the gaping customers. I gestured to the table next to me. "I'm bringing Polly."

"Oh, brother," she sighed.

Hamson's clean-cut jaw ticked as he watched James leave. Then he turned his gaze back on me. "A date?"

"It's not a date."

Hamson scoffed as he turned away. "Didn't know you had a thing for guys with man buns."

Chapter Two

"ALL I'M SAYING IS that if Hamson left without a bagel, it means he was there to see *you*." Verity adjusted Pooh Bear's leash to keep him from pulling too far ahead. As it was, people cleared the sidewalk when they saw my giant German Shepherd coming, never mind that he was my cuddly pooch.

But not as cuddly as my new puppy, Cujo—a recent gift from Hamson. The golden fluff ball hated to be separated from me, which was why his little head was now poking out of my handbag as we walked across Beaver Bluff's town square. It was only the second time I'd seen Verity over the last few days since my close encounter with Hamson and James's sudden appearance. She'd been spending most of her time with David, her new boyfriend, whose grandmother's murder we'd recently solved.

"If Hamson was there to see me, he wouldn't have walked right back out the door." The memory, only thirty minutes old, still stung. I quickened my steps, trying to keep warm against the brisk wind. Just days ago, the autumn leaves had turned and fallen to the ground, but winter was already sweeping in, making my preferred fashion choice of flirty sundresses and heels hard to justify. Not that it stopped me.

"Maybe you should have gone after him." Verity swiped a

stray strand of red hair away from her face, then she zeroed in on me with a sharp gaze. "Unless he was right to be jealous. Are you sure you're over James?"

My nose wrinkled. "Duh. There's nothing that man could do that would lure me back to him or to LA." Although that last point was still in the air. While I loved being home in Beaver Bluff, it was definitely harder for a former social media manager to make a living in a small town.

Verity tugged Pooh Bear's leash, and we came to a stop. "But does Hamson know that?"

Maybe not. The truth was, I'd wanted to follow Hamson when he left Crumb's, but doing so would have given off desperation vibes. And what would be a worse turnoff than that? Still, I needed to get through to him…in a non-desperate vibey way.

"I'll think about it." I gently drew Cujo out of my bag and handed him over to Verity. "In the meantime, I have a new customer to land." I nodded toward Wilson's Jewelers, located near the self-defense dojo that Verity frequented.

"Can you make it quick? David and I have a late lunch scheduled."

My heart sank, but I tried to keep my expression neutral. Just like Polly was feeling a little left out by Naomi and Walter's new relationship, I was feeling left out by Verity and David. Of *course*, I wanted my bestie to have the love of her dreams, especially after she canceled her wedding to some loser a few months back, but at the same time, I was just settling into the rhythm of having a close friend.

I mustered a smile. "I'll try to hurry."

My phone chimed, as did Verity's from the pocket of her flannel shirt. "Must be one of the gang," she said, referring to our group chat. "You'll have to check since my hands are full." She gestured to the dogs.

I pulled out my phone. "It's from Naomi."

Verity hovered over my shoulder to get a look. "What's it say?"

I swiped open the text, which had a fuzzy photo of Naomi

and Walter grinning, with her left hand held high. "Oh, wow." I reread the words to make sure I didn't imagine them. "It says they're engaged and getting married as soon as possible."

NOT GONNA LIE–I was still a little shaken by Naomi's news when I approached the jewelry store. Not that I didn't like her new fiancé. In fact, I thought he was pretty great, even though I'd once had a tiny suspicion he could be a murderer. It was the warp speed of the engagement that had me concerned.

But instead of dwelling on a situation over which I had zero control, I composed my thoughts, pasted on a smile, and strode inside the store. Track lighting on the ceiling illuminated the glass cases that jutted out from three of the four walls. Behind the longest case stood a middle-aged gentleman wearing a flannel vest —who even knew there was such a thing?—over a dress shirt, assisting a shaggy blond male customer who vibrated with nervous energy.

"I'll be with you in a moment," said the man behind the counter. Based on his website photo, I knew him to be Randall, the store's owner.

I offered a small wave before turning to the display case near the window that contained a few dazzling pieces that were likely costume, considering their proximity to the door. Despite the relative safety of Beaver Bluff—the recent murders notwithstanding— no jewelry store owner in their right mind would keep their valuables handy for a smash-and-grab thief. I perused the sparkling bracelets merchandised on rustic wood jewelry displays while the men finished up. The store itself was a strange mixture of glitz and timber.

"I'm sure she'll love the ring you've selected." The vested man handed over a small bag.

The customer let out a whoosh of air while cracking his neck and adjusting his work shirt. "I can't believe I'm finally going to ask her. It's all good, though. I mean, she's going to say yes."

"Let me offer my hearty congratulations ahead of time, Phil." The man behind the counter smiled pleasantly. "In any case, maybe I'll see you at tomorrow night's get-together at the B&B?"

"Yeah, with everything else going on, I almost forgot. Not sure I'm going to make it." The excited soon-to-be-fiancé slid on a pair of sunglasses. "Wish me luck." He held the bag up in a mock toast, then tipped his chin up as he said goodbye.

"You're going to the party tomorrow too?" I asked as soon as the vested gentleman and I were alone.

A momentary frown creased his face before he caught himself and smiled. "I'm sorry. Have we met?"

I extended my hand across the counter. "KC Crumb."

"That's right. I didn't realize it was already time for our appointment." His face relaxed, giving me a chance to study the fine lines around his eyes, lines that belied his thick, jet-black hair.

"If it's not a good time, I can come back." *Please don't say yes. Please don't say yes.* While I wanted to be accommodating, I had a schedule to keep if I wanted to grow my business.

"Now is fine." He folded his hands on the case. "As you were saying, you're going to the gathering tomorrow night? I had no idea you were associated with Benson Michaels and Associates."

The name struck a chord, but I couldn't remember why. "Benson Michaels?"

"Yes, the law firm hosting the party."

"Oh, that's right." I remembered their firm from the murder we'd recently investigated. "I'm not associated with them. I'm doing a job for the B&B, so I'll be there to observe."

His eyebrow quirked.

"What?" I asked.

"Nothing, nothing," he chuckled. "I'm looking forward to the party."

What was with the weird eyebrow thing? I wanted to push for an answer, but I wanted him as a client more, so I decided not to go there. Aunt Lulu would be proud of me for staying out of something that was clearly not my business.

I set my bag on the counter. "How are you associated with Benson Michaels?"

"My wife Brenda works there." Randall grinned. "Fabulous firm."

I remembered my previous interactions with Brenda, a secretary for the law firm, who seemed like a genuinely nice lady. "Should be a fun evening." Actually, I had no idea if it would be or not, but if I got to the B&B in time this afternoon, I could offer whatever advice I could come up with before the event.

"Unfortunately, my sales associate called in sick today, so it's just me running the store." Randall glanced around, as if to confirm he was without backup. "I'm afraid we'll have to have our meeting right here."

"That's fine. I don't mind." I pulled my tablet out of my handbag and booted up. "First, I'm interested in how you learned about my services."

Randall chuckled. "Have you heard your aunt and her friends talk about you?"

Indeed, I had. Heat crept up my neck and settled in my cheeks. "Sometimes they have a tendency to oversell. Not that I'm not as good as they said," I was quick to add.

"I get it. They can be a..." Randall hesitated, glancing skyward. "Persuasive bunch." That was putting it mildly.

"Believe me, I know." I opened a fresh spreadsheet. "Now, tell me what kind of work you're hoping to have me do."

He shrugged, which seemed incongruent with the polished salesman from moments ago. "Help me get the store off the ground, so to speak. I haven't had much luck with advertising, although I have sold some beautiful pieces over the last few days."

Maybe one of those beautiful pieces included the giant rock on Naomi's left ring finger. I took another gander around the sales floor. "You have a lot of nice displays. Have you highlighted any of these on your social channels?"

Randall tilted his head. "Social channels?"

I nodded, waiting for him to continue.

"Forgive me, but I'm just not sure what that means."

I clutched my chest. "Sorry. Sometimes I forget that not everyone lives and breathes social media the way I do. Your social channels are the social media outlets you've chosen to use to promote your brand."

"Brand?"

"You know, your store's image." Which, as I looked around, appeared to be lumberjack chic—just like the rest of Beaver Bluff.

Randall's face wrinkled. "I'm really not into that image stuff. I enjoy selling nice jewelry at reasonable prices."

"Totally, totally." I nodded, trying to figure out a way to slowly rebrand the store into something that at least agreed with itself. Either be rustic and gritty or be chic. It was impossible to be both. And I had a feeling I knew which brand Beaver Bluffians would go for. "We'll work with what you've got going, plus we can incorporate some new ideas."

Randall held up a hand. "Wait, now. I don't really want to mess with the store. I like it the way it is."

And yet he could make a killing if he let me make a few changes. However, that wasn't the business I was in. I needed to promote his store for what it was. "Great!" I said, more enthusiastically than I felt. "We'll go with lumberjack chic."

"What?"

"Nothing." I waved him off. "Just leave it to me. We'll pick one social media platform to build and work from there." I tapped a few notes on my tablet. "Now, do you have any upcoming events we can promote?"

"Events? No, not really. I mean, every year we do a winter thingy."

"Thingy?" This time it was my turn to question, as I did not specialize in thingies.

For the next half hour or so, Randall and I went back and forth, massaging his ideas into something palatable. The "winter thingy" turned into an "extravaganza," and we chose a platform to build based on the store's demographics. Next, we looked at his customer file—I was proud that I didn't peek to see if Walter and Naomi were in there—and talked about starting a newsletter with the smattering of email addresses he'd gathered since opening. After that, I took some photos I'd use to build the store's profile.

After discussing my fees, I tucked my tablet back inside my handbag. "I think that's about all we need to get started."

"Thank you. I think this is really going to work out." Randall nodded with appreciation as he walked me to the door. "So, I guess I'll see you tomorrow night?"

"Huh? Oh, the party. Yes, I'll be there." I pushed against the door handle.

"You said you're doing some work for the B&B? Is it the same kind you just did for me?" Randall's eyebrow quirked again.

I hesitated. "That's right. Basically the same, but I tweak my approach for each business."

Randall's mouth puckered. "Hmm. Just a word of caution, then." He poised his finger to his lips. "Make sure to get your payment up front."

Chapter Three

THE JEWELER'S words echoed inside my head as I walked one street north of the town square toward the Beaver Bluff Bed and Breakfast. If I were a woman of good judgment, I'd probably turn around and forget about landing the account.

However, there was no way I could shun Mason and still save face in front of James after they'd done the man-bonding thing back at the bakery. Besides, going to tomorrow night's soiree would give me a legitimate reason to talk to James and convince him to leave town. The sooner he left, the sooner I could get back to whatever it was Antonio Hamson and I had started.

Despite Verity's protests, I'd persuaded her to keep my pups until I was done with this appointment. David wouldn't mind the dogs joining them for their late lunch, as he was still in the impressing-his-new-girlfriend's-friends phase of the relationship.

The B&B was a three-story Victorian-style home, complete with a gabled roof, a turret, and a wrap-around porch. Two smaller homes sat jealously on either side of it. The neighborhood itself was modest and occupied mostly by long-term, older residents who prided themselves on tidy yards and a quiet life. (Except for Polly, who lived around the corner and was anything but quiet.)

I parked behind a white van and sat for a moment. I mentally rehearsed my pitch as I walked up the cobblestone path and ascended the steps leading up to the porch. Ceramic vases full of flowers too bright to be real this time of year framed the front door, which squawked in protest when I opened it. Unlike the outside of the house, the inside appeared less authentic, as though it had undergone a recent renovation. The foyer led to an open-concept combined lobby and living area, while straight ahead, a long counter sectioned off the dining room. Beyond that was a swinging door that likely led to the kitchen. Apart from the counter and barstools, the furniture and décor reflected the era, from what little I knew about it.

Terse voices carried from a hallway to the left.

"Hello?" I called meekly, unsure whether I wanted to interrupt.

The conversation continued between a man who wasn't shy about being overhead and a soft-spoken woman. Mason and his sister Dana? Or maybe it was two B&B guests. I strained to hear both sides.

"You people were told to provide payment upon service." The deep voice, who was definitely not Mason, boomed. "I took this job in good faith after the last incident."

I stifled a gasp. The accusation lined up with exactly what Randall, the jeweler, had warned me about. Quietly, I edged toward the hallway, grateful for the thick mulberry-colored rug that covered the faux-wood floor. The woman responded too quietly for me to make out the words, which was rather unfair since I wanted to hear what she had to say.

"Tell your brother to pony up," the man responded. "Remember, it's a small town. Word gets around." Angry footsteps thudded closer.

Quickly, I scurried back towards the front door and pretended I'd just walked in. "Hello?" I called out loudly.

The unshaven man with grizzly graying hair emerged from the hallway, looked at me, and stormed toward the back of the house. Seconds later, a woman appeared, her face inflamed with emotion. "Electricians, am I right?" She issued a nervous chuckle.

"For sure." I matched her chuckle with one of my own, though I literally had no idea what it was like to work with an electrician. I stuck out my hand. "I'm KC Crumb. Did your brother tell you I'd be stopping by?"

Uncertainty flickered across the woman's tired face before she recovered and offered a smile. She appeared to be in her mid-thirties and looked nothing like her brother Mason, though, to be fair, his bushy mustache made it hard to compare. She tucked a wavy strand of brown hair behind her ear. "I don't believe Mason said anything. How can I help you?"

"Actually, I'm here to see if I can help *you*."

"Are you the caterer?"

"No, do you need one?" I added caterer to the mental checklist I was already starting. Even though the party was tomorrow, perhaps the gang and I could whip up a few hors d'oeuvres and desserts.

Except, the B&B seemed to have a problem paying up.

"I do, since my oven is on the fritz, or maybe it's just the electricity. But I've already put in a call to a caterer that came recommended. Thanks, anyway." She hesitated before speaking softly again. "What is it you're here for?"

"To offer you a consultation, starting with tomorrow night's party." I'd have offered her a business card if I'd had one. I added that to my mental checklist, too.

She straightened and fisted her hands on her waist. "He told you I needed help, did he?"

"Not exactly. You see, I consult with local businesses on their social media, branding, promotions, events—those types of things. So, when I talked to your brother earlier at the bakery, I thought maybe I could—"

"You met at a bakery?"

"It was the end of my shift, and I was—"

"You *work* at a bakery?"

"No, yes…it's a long story."

Dana grimaced. "I don't think I need a baker to help with my event."

"Trust me, I'm not a baker."

"That's too bad for the bakery."

I swished my hands in front of me, as if to clear the air. "Let me start over. I do consulting work for businesses, and I'd like to see if we could help raise your profile to become the premier B&B of the Pacific Northwest." My hand panned the sky, as if painting a vision for the future.

James's voice sounded from the staircase on the opposite side of the room. "And she *is* the best."

Then why did you fire me?

James descended the last few steps. A cocky grin spread across his face as he sauntered across the room with an irritating level of confidence.

"Mr. Carlisle, I hope you like your accommodations." Dana flashed a professional smile, a lot bigger than the one she'd offered me. No surprise, though, as James tended to have that effect on people, especially women.

"Nice room, a view of the ocean—what more could I ask for?" James folded his arms across his chest.

"I take it you two know each other?" Dana pointed between James and me.

"Know each other?" He palmed my shoulder. "We go way back. We used to—"

"Work together," I finished.

James cleared his throat. "And like I said, she's the best." He took his sunglasses off his head and slid them over his eyes as he headed for the door. At the last second, he turned to me. "I'll be seeing you." He pointed his finger at me like a fake gun.

I cocked my own fake gun and shot him back.

"Well, well," Dana sighed. "As it happens, I do need a little extra help. Tomorrow night's party didn't come together quite like I thought it would with my oven situation and whatnot. The law firm I'm hosting had some decorating ideas, but they fell through on their end. And of course, my part-time worker is out sick."

"Ouch, sounds like you have your hands full."

"That's an understatement."

"Don't worry about a thing." I pulled my tablet out of my handbag. "I don't want to toot my own horn, but party planning is kind of a specialty of mine."

Dana's rigid posture relaxed, and she nodded appreciatively as she let out a long breath. "I'm not even sure where to start. The law firm only came to me a week ago, and I thought I could make it happen, but you know how it goes." She led me to a decorative wooden bar top near the fireplace that she likely used for checking in guests. Or maybe as an actual bar.

I powered up the tablet. "Let's make a list of all the essentials."

For the next ten minutes, I queried Dana about the event, the number of guests, and her client's expectations. Then I made a list of action items that included tasks she'd already completed. She struck me as the type who would appreciate seeing some boxes already checked off.

"That should be enough to get you organized." I added a header to the document, using a logo for my business that I'd experimented with for the last few days. "Would you like me to email this to you?"

"I'd prefer a hard copy, if you don't mind." Dana appeared to be a few years younger than me, which put her around thirty-five. Definitely young enough that it surprised me she preferred paper.

"Sure." I hit the print icon and selected the B&B's printer. "It should be coming right up. Where's your printer?" I tucked my tablet back inside my handbag.

"It's just down the hall, in my office." Dana pointed in the direction that she and the angry man had emerged from earlier. As she led the way to the office space in the turret, I again wondered how I was going to get paid.

If only James hadn't been around this morning, I would have

been able to walk away from this without worrying about losing face in front of him. The question was, why did I care so much about what he thought? It certainly wasn't due to lingering romantic feelings. I guess I wanted him to see me as having landed on my feet.

When we entered the turret, which may have formerly been a small parlor, the printer finished spitting out a page. Then, on the corner of her desk, a screen caught my eye. It was a live video feed of the front room.

Heat rushed to my cheeks when I realized there was no way Dana and the electrician hadn't known I was there before I pretended like I'd just walked in. Maybe Verity was right—honesty was always better than deceit.

Dana picked up the checklist and nodded. "This looks great. I knew most of this, but I'd forgotten about the music. What you've added is going to take the party up a level."

I beamed. "That's what I do." I patted my handbag that held my tablet. "And I have my part, too. I'll be here before the party tomorrow to help with the finishing touches."

Out in the front room, the door creaked open, and someone walked in. "Hello?"

"Be right there." Dana motioned for me to leave the office before her.

When I emerged from the short hall, a short young brunette with a T-shirt that read Carla's Catering and More waited by the door. Briefly, I wondered what the "and More" stood for. Although, considering what I was doing for a living, I probably needed a business card that said the same thing.

"I'll be in touch." I smiled at Dana, nodded at the caterer, then walked out the front door.

Where I ran right into Mason.

"Watch out there, little lady." He grasped my shoulders, though I was in no danger of falling.

I quickly broke away from his touch and did everything I could to rein in my expression. "I'm fine, thanks," I said through gritted teeth, noting how Mason's eyes traveled over me. If I hadn't already met with Dana, I would chuck this job regardless of what James thought.

Mason tipped his imaginary hat and walked inside, closing the door with a soft click.

"I don't like the way he looks at you." James's voice sounded behind me.

"Stop sneaking up on me." I clutched my chest as I turned and looked at James, rocking gently on the porch swing.

"No one is sneaking. I'm sitting here enjoying the view I paid for." He stood and let the swing continue on without him. "What I'm not liking is the way that man was ogling you."

I shrugged to cede the point. "Too bad you recommended me so highly to him, otherwise, I wouldn't even be here."

"Just trying to help you out, although I'm having second thoughts."

"You're the whole reason I'm in Beaver Bluff in the first place." I descended the stairs in a huff.

Sadly, he followed. "I made some mistakes, and I'm here to make them right. You don't need to be working with people like this jerk."

I paused and turned slowly to face James. "It's too late. You really just need to go back to California and let me get on with my life."

"Not until we talk—I mean, *really* talk." His eyes pleaded.

A stiff wind whipped up around us. I caught my dress to keep it from flying up. "Look, I get that you're sorry. Whatever. The point is, I'm over it. And after tomorrow night's party, I don't expect to see you again."

"About that…maybe you shouldn't come to the party."

"What?" I shook my head to clear my muddled thoughts. "I have to be here. I gave my word. And if *they* don't pay up, *you* promised to." I smirked at the thought.

A dark look clouded James's face. He glanced over his shoulder, then fixed his gaze back on me. "I think I was wrong to get you involved here. I have a bad feeling about that dude."

On that, we agreed.

Chapter Four

DESPITE RECENTLY SAMPLING ALL the pastries at Crumb's—mostly for quality control purposes—I could still fit into a dress that James once said made me look like a knockout. When I picked up Polly before the party, she accused me of donning the little black dress just to impress him. And she wasn't wrong. Even though I wanted nothing more to do with James, I still wanted him to live with lifelong pain and regret for his bad choices.

However, the dress was not conducive to crawling around on the floor, which was where I found myself shortly before the guests were due to arrive for the evening soiree at the B&B. I crouched behind a counter that would double as a sound booth—if I could get the rented sound system working.

What I needed was better light. The sun had almost set, and it was a moonless night, which didn't matter anyway since I was in the dead center of the house where outside light didn't reach. I used the flashlight on my phone to try to make sense of the plugs and switches.

"Maybe you should try doing something with that one." Polly pointed to a dangling wire that seemingly had no place to go.

I snarled.

"Just trying to help. But never mind." She held up her hands. "So…what do you think about Naomi's news?"

I stopped messing with the sound system and considered her question. "Honestly, I'm a little surprised. It seemed like that's where she and Walter were heading, but I just thought they would take time to get to know each other first."

"At our age, you can't afford to wait."

I studied Polly's downcast face. "Are you okay with it?"

"Of course. I was getting tired of spending so much time with her, anyway." Her voice faltered. "I'll just go check out the food. Looks like shish kebabs are on the menu. They've got an indoor grill and everything." Even in the low light, the sequins on her black pantsuit shimmered as she backed away toward the kitchen.

Alone, I sat in an unladylike manner and started googling directions. Perhaps I shouldn't have suggested setting up a sound system for music and mics in the first place, but it seemed like a glaring omission for a party.

Footsteps followed by whispers sounded from the other side of the counter that sectioned off the front room from the dining area. People were coming down the stairs.

"I told him to pay me half up front, and now I'm worried I won't get paid at all. Then I'll be out the cost of the food plus my time." The first voice had to be Carla, the caterer.

I held my breath and strained to hear the other person, who spoke even more softly.

"I tried to warn you." It was difficult to tell if the voice was male or female. "Even if the lawyer pays him, it doesn't mean he'll pay you."

"You're the one who got me this gig," Carla said with a peevish tone.

"Don't worry. Mark my words, Mason will get what's coming to him." The person paused. "Some guy almost came to blows with him earlier today. Trust me, no one likes him."

What on earth? Apparently, I wasn't the only person who wasn't a fan of the mustachioed B&B owner. My prospects for getting a regular ongoing client out of this night grew dimmer by the second. Maybe Polly had the right idea to load up on the free food.

Footsteps sounded over the faux-wood flooring as the pair broke apart. Quickly, I busied myself with the dangling wire as someone approached the counter where I was currently hiding. No, wait. I was *working*, with a perfect right to be where I was.

Carla gasped when she saw me. "Oh, I didn't know anyone was here."

Clearly.

I held up the wire and smiled. "Just trying to get the sound system ready. Hey, I hear you've got shish kebabs on the menu. Sounds great."

She offered a tight smile, then adjusted her apron before retreating to the kitchen area behind me. Hopefully, Polly hadn't sampled too much of the food, or Carla would be even more upset.

Minutes later, the first guests started to arrive, just as I finished following a YouTube tutorial to set up the sound system. Dana swept into the room, her brown hair in a beautiful updo, while her clothing was more demure and businesslike. On her heels was her brother, dressed the same way he was yesterday, in boring khakis. While Dana worked the room, ensuring everyone's comfort, Mason stood between the front room and the dining area, checking his watch and looking agitated.

It didn't take long for the front room to fill with people and for the party to get underway. Sometimes I missed the gatherings and soirees from my former life, but on the whole, Beaver Bluff was turning out to be a great move. And if I could help the town step up their social game, I'd consider it a job well done.

I stood near the staircase and congratulated myself for the ideas I'd contributed. In addition to the sound system, I'd convinced Dana to set up high-top tables throughout the front room and a backdrop for photo-ops, which now had a line of people dressed in sparkling dresses and eveningwear. The rest of the crowd started congregating around the indoor grill in the dining area, waiting for their food. Carla, the caterer, appeared harried as she bounced between the kitchen and dining area, working the line.

So far, there was no sign of James. Thank heaven for small favors.

"This is quite the shindig." Randall, the jeweler, toasted me with his glass.

I toasted him back with my plate full of shish kebab that I'd nearly nicked myself assembling. I also loaded up on dessert items that I felt the need to sample as competitive research for Crumb's. "This is quite the turnout." I elevated my voice to speak over the music, which I probably needed to turn down a skosh. "I had no idea so many people worked for Benson Michaels."

He took a swig of his drink. "I don't think everyone here does. Looks like they invited a lot of extra people."

The crowd had grown. Even though there were only thirty or so people present, it seemed like more, considering the size of the room. "Which one is Benson?"

Randall pointed to a tall African American gentleman taking turns with people for their selfies in front of a festive backdrop. "Looks like he spared no expense this evening."

"Work hard, play hard," Brenda, Randall's wife and a secretary at the law firm, said as she joined us. "It's our motto."

"Say cheese." I snapped a few pictures with my phone to use for the B&B's social media while we chatted. Then the couple left to mingle with Brenda's coworkers. It gave me a chance to tuck into the dessert without stopping to speak…until I was joined by Griff, my sometimes-personal trainer.

Quickly, I tried to ditch the plate, but not before he tsked me.

"KC, great to see you." Griff toasted me with what I was certain was a low-calorie no-flavor mocktail. Briefly, he eyed my plate.

I swallowed without chewing, filling myself with empty carbs and regret. I barely got to taste the chocolate bits. "Fancy seeing you here."

"Guess where else you'll be seeing me?" His eyes gleamed.

I winced. "At the gym in the morning?"

"Bingo." He nodded and chuckled.

"Hi, I'm James. And you are?" James stepped between us and held out his hand.

"Griff." He didn't miss a beat or appear as put off as I felt by James's intrusion. "I'm KC's personal trainer. She does pretty well...*when* she makes it in." He winked and turned away, joined by his fiancée, Holly.

"Dude's pretty buff." James gawked at Griff, as most people did the first time they met him, and saw that even his muscles had muscles.

I grabbed my plate and resumed sampling the dessert. "Thought maybe I'd gotten lucky and you'd found something else to do tonight."

He leaned in and shoulder bumped me, the scent of his exotic cologne wafting over me in irritating waves. It didn't help that he was wearing dark slacks and a sweater that brought out the gold flecks in his eyes. "You know I like to make an entrance." He tightened his man bun.

I snorted. "Sadly for you, no one here cares, including me." Saying mean words didn't feel as good as I thought, but I refused to apologize.

"Well, you *should* care that I'm here." His tone took a serious turn.

"Why? There really isn't anything to say. I'm not going back with you. My life is here now." Mostly. I still nurtured the fantasy of escaping back into the bustling California life—if my business didn't take off.

"It's not about that." His jaw flexed. "It's about him." He chin-motioned toward Mason across the room.

"What are you talking about?" I spoke as softly as I could over the music and the people who'd formed a conga line that snaked between the tables. I snapped a few more pics.

"Just about knocked that dude out this afternoon." He pounded his fist into his other hand.

The Bavarian cream-filled puff went down the wrong way, causing me to cough. "That was you? I overheard people talking about that. What happened?" Despite my ill feelings toward James, he'd always been a laid-back person, more likely to tell someone to take a chill pill than to need one himself.

James drew a deep breath, his gaze turning to steel. "Let's just say he made some comments you wouldn't appreciate."

"Huh?"

"Comments about you and your…" He motioned to my body, up and down. "You, he made lewd comments about *you*." James shot a laser-like glare across the room. "I told him where he could stuff—"

"I can't believe this." My stomach roiled with rage. "Who does that man think he is? That does it. I don't need clients like him." I would leave just as soon as I pocketed a few more puffs.

"What's going on?" Polly joined us, concern lining her face.

James attempted to placate her with a calming hand. "Nothing for you to worry about."

Polly straightened. "I can decide that for myself, thank you very much." Her jowls trembled when she spoke.

I hesitated to fill Polly in. No question, she'd teach Mason a lesson he'd never forget and probably land herself in jail. "James had a problem this afternoon with—"

"The dude is staring at us right now." James's eyes were fixed across the room, despite the conga line winding its way between Mason and us on the other side. "He's actually leering at you."

"Ignore him. Just…check out of here and go home," I urged. James leaving town would solve multiple problems. He was the only reason I almost took the B&B owners on as clients in the first place. But I was about to rectify that problem.

"I tried. He wouldn't give me my money back." James's eyes slivered.

Jerk. His refusal to give the money back was affecting me now, too.

Mason turned away and headed through the dining area toward the kitchen.

"I'm going to talk to him again. He doesn't want a piece of this action." James straightened and dusted off his sleeves.

Polly rolled her eyes.

"I'll be right back." James disappeared into a swell of people doing the bunny hop.

"Don't do anything I wouldn't do, blah blah," I half-heartedly called after him. I turned to Polly. "Did you try the puffs?"

"To die for." Polly nodded. "Maybe Lulu could add something like this to the menu."

"I was just thinking that." I popped the last one into my mouth. "Let's grab a few more, then we can get out of here."

"Wait, I thought you were working." She air-quoted the last word.

"Not after what James told me." I glanced around, wishing I could just do business with Dana instead of having to deal with her brother, too. This would've been a sweet gig, and I had *so* many ideas for helping the B&B. "Anyway, let's get more food, and we'll leave."

Polly shrugged. "That's fine. If we leave now, I can still make it to bingo."

All at once, the lights cut out, and the music stopped. People groaned, and everyone's voices chimed in to ask what happened. I willed my eyes to adjust, but it was pitch black. I reached out and felt for Polly's shoulder. Judging by the number of sequins, I'd grabbed the right person. "Don't move. I'm sure the lights will be back in a minute."

"Come on, who's the joker who cut the music?" someone called from the crowd.

"You're the only joker here."

The crowd laughed.

"Who needs music to bunny hop?"

"Literally everyone."

More laughter.

"Music? What about the lights?"

A clatter sounded from the kitchen area. People stopped murmuring. Then there was another clatter, followed by a loud thump. I tensed and gripped Polly's shoulder more tightly as my eyes scanned the room. It was still too dark to see.

"Okay, this isn't funny anymore."

"Duh, it never was."

Nervous chuckles rumbled through the crowd.

I reached for my phone and switched on the flashlight, wondering why no one had thought of it before. "Does anyone know where the fuse box is?"

More phone lights flicked on. The beam swept over the front room, illuminating an increasingly anxious crowd.

"Everyone, stay calm." Dana's voice trembled. "We've had electrical trouble lately. We'll get it fixed in a jiffy."

"Probably had the electricity turned off," an anonymous voice chided.

With the phone held in front of me, I pressed through the crowd, Polly on my heels. We made it to Dana on the other side of the room. "Let's get to the fuse box, and we'll get back up and running." Then Polly and I could leave and get on with our night.

"This way." Dana brought me to her side, ushering me toward the kitchen.

The beam of light swept across the floor just in front of us, landing on a crumpled figure. My pulse skidded to a stop. I gasped, and the light jerked to the ceiling as I covered my mouth.

"What?" Polly's voice cut through the dark.

Beams of light approached behind us as the crowd pressed closer.

I aimed the light back at the motionless figure, dressed in khaki, sprawled face-up on the floor between the kitchen and the dining area. Mason's open eyes didn't blink but remained fixed on the ceiling, and a skewer protruded from his chest. A crimson stain spread across his shirt, announcing what we already knew.

Dana's scream rent the air as the crowd pressed closer. Her terrified voice broke over the commotion. "Call nine-one-one!"

People panicked, and shrieks sounded from one end of the room to the other. I stood frozen, with Mason trapped in my beam of light.

Polly gripped my arm and gasped. "Death, by shish kebab."

Chapter Five

SCREAMS ECHOED THROUGH THE B&B, but none louder than mine.

It doesn't matter how many times one discovers a dead body —for me, this was number three—it's still horrifying. My stomach roiled, and I fought to calm myself.

Dana's knees buckled. I dropped my phone as I reached out to catch her before she hit the floor next to her brother. Behind us, a cacophony erupted as everyone dialed nine-one-one at the same time. I guided Dana to a nearby chair in the dining area and angled her away from the body.

"What…what…I don't…" Dana stuttered incoherently.

"Take a deep breath. The police are on the way." I was reassuring myself as much as her.

Polly leaned over and felt his neck. "Yep, he's a goner."

"Polly!" I motioned for her to back off from the body. "Get away from the…" I lowered my voice. "You-know-what."

She shrugged, unshaken by the situation. "I had to check, just in case there was *something* we could still do for him." At least someone was thinking clearly.

"The police are on their way." Benson Michaels tucked his phone inside his suit pocket, an air of calm surrounding him. "What we need right now is for everyone to step back this way so we don't contaminate the scene." He ushered the crowd toward the front room. "That's right, everyone come this way. We'll get it all sorted out."

Despite the fact that Benson was an estate attorney and didn't practice criminal law, he seemed to know what he was doing. I was grateful for the calm he added to the situation and found myself relaxing a fraction.

"The police have requested that everyone stay on the property," he instructed.

"I think Charmin already left," someone said. "But maybe that was *before*."

"Well, *that* seems suspicious."

"Are we all going to suspect each other now?"

People murmured their concerns.

"Wait, do you think this was done on purpose?" A woman with hair in a sleek chignon asked.

"Obviously."

"He didn't do that to himself."

"Thanks, Sherlock." This, from someone who apparently appreciated gallows humor.

I glanced back at Mason, noting his position as best I could from the scant light of other people's phones. Clearly, he'd stumbled through the doorway between the kitchen and the dining area, and the thump we'd heard was him landing on his back. Had he died instantly? It was hard to say, considering it took us a few minutes after the lights went off to discover him. Despite the shock, I mentally cataloged the position of the body and tried to recall as many details as I could about what happened just before the lights went out.

Polly handed my phone to me, then she picked up a plate off the table and loaded it with lemon tarts.

"Have some respect." I glanced back and forth between Dana and Polly, hoping she'd get the hint.

Polly grabbed one more tart, then backed away and was absorbed into the crowd.

Dana shook her head. "It's…it's okay."

Nothing was okay, actually, but I wasn't going to argue with the victim's sister. Instead, I patted her shoulder, wishing I had a blanket to wrap around her like they did on TV. "Would you like to move to another room?"

She covered her face with her hands. "No, I just…I can't leave him."

I questioned her decision but said nothing. Soon enough, the police would clear the scene, and she'd have to move. I glanced at the partygoers, who had stopped training their phone lights on the body and started focusing on each other. They all spoke in hushed tones as they tried to account for one another and themselves.

"I was in the conga line, right behind Bob."

"That was you?" a man wearing a rhinestone tiara asked. "I thought that was Beverly."

"No, I was in front of you, Bob," a woman said.

"Are you sure?" he asked.

"Looks like Bob hit the punchbowl a few too many times."

The crowd chuckled but then seemed to catch themselves being irreverent.

"So, it was Jeremy, Beverly, Bob, Susan, then who?" Brenda started pointing to different people, then waiting for their responses before continuing. "I think everyone who was in the conga line is accounted for."

More people chimed in, saying they were in the line as well. Even though the conga had been long, I was pretty sure it didn't include everyone in the room. But I could see their point—no one wanted to be accused of the murder, and as long as someone could prove they were in the conga line, they were safe.

"Obviously, the murderer is that one man," said someone in the crowd.

"Who?" Several people, including Griff and Holly, echoed the question as they shined their lights, trying to locate the person who'd made the accusation.

"The guy with the man bun." The faceless person spoke

again.

"James," I breathed his name. Frantically, I glanced around for my ex. Where was he? I rose, leaving Dana behind me as I broke into the crowd. "Who said that?" I shined my light from face to face, but no one fessed up. "Does anyone know who said that?"

Everyone looked at one another, but no one admitted they'd accused James. Instead, they started questioning each other about who had a man bun and where this person was.

I willed James to appear in the crowd and defend himself. While he'd admitted to arguing with Mason earlier, there was no way he'd have done the deed. If there was anyone who could stomach a dead body less than me, it was James.

"It's true. They had a nasty fight earlier, and I saw him follow Mason a few minutes ago," Dana's voice quivered. We all turned to look at her as she used the table to steady herself when she stood. "James Carlisle is the killer."

IT DIDN'T TAKE LONG for Beaver Bluff's men and women in blue, including Officer Hamson, to arrive along with the county coroner and cordon off the bed-and-breakfast. The firetruck and ambulance came too, but there was nothing they could do for Mason. They did, however, give Dana oxygen and a foil blanket.

The police took a quick headcount before requiring us to wait in the front yard, though I was almost certain a few people had left the premises. The rest of us huddled under patio lamps that Benson Michaels had convinced one of the officers to bring around from the back. Thankfully, someone had gotten the electricity back on so we wouldn't have to wait in the dark. Instead, we had the overhead porch lights and the twinkle lights strung around the front garden.

One by one, the police took each partygoer to one of two secluded spots on the wraparound porch. They were to speak with either Hamson or his partner, Officer Leon, an African American woman whose beautiful eyelashes I coveted. Meanwhile, a man named Officer Ryan babysat those of us left to wait, trying to keep us from talking. Because of my previous involvements in recent murder cases, through no fault of my own, I was pretty familiar with the entirety of the small police force.

Polly shivered, despite the enormity of her puffy coat. "You'd think they'd let an old lady go home," she said, her voice feeble.

"If there were an old lady here, they probably would," I called her bluff.

"Fine, but I wish they'd hurry up. It's past my bedtime."

"It's not even nine o'clock." I glanced at my phone to make certain I was right. "Whichever one of us gets done first needs to call the gang together." I leaned close and whispered. "We have a lot to discuss."

"Hey, let's stop the chatter." Officer Ryan pointed at us.

Polly scowled at him, causing the young officer to look away first. Perhaps that was why she was called next, and I shortly thereafter. I was led to the right side of the Victorian home, where a small workstation was set up. As much as I'd wanted to see Antonio Hamson, these weren't the circumstances I'd had in mind. I took a seat across from him, taking a moment to appreciate his strong presence, the cut of his jaw, and the faint scent of his cologne. Maybe tonight, we could finally talk and get reconnected.

Static from the radio on Hamson's shoulder squawked. He made a note on the small computer perched on a TV tray that doubled as his table. Hamson spoke without looking at me. "Another murder in Beaver Bluff, and here you are at the center of it, just like before."

So much for making a connection.

I shivered against the night air but refused to look as vulnerable as I felt, just like I refused to acknowledge his ridiculous comment. He knew good and well that I just happened to be at the wrong place at the wrong time with the previous murders, and this one would prove to be the same.

The wicker chair creaked as I leaned back and crossed my legs (that happened to look pretty good in this dress, according to previous comments made by James, who was still mysteriously missing. But I couldn't dwell on that bit.)

Hamson cleared his throat and finally looked up and saw me. His gaze swept over me, warming me from the inside, causing my heart to stutter. But he quickly shifted into investigation mode. "Well?"

"Well, what?" I lifted my hand and casually gazed at my fingernails as though I hadn't a care in the world. "You're the one conducting the interview. So…" I waved my hand with flair. "Conduct."

Hamson released a deep groan. "Oh, come on. Cut the—"

"Hey now." I sat up and spoke through gritted teeth. "You're the one who tried to insinuate that I have something to do with all this stuff going on."

"It just so happens that—" As quickly as his professional veneer had dropped, it went back up. His expression slid back into cop mode as he informed me I was being recorded. Then he started with the questioning. "Where were you when the lights went out?"

"Wouldn't you like to know?" I smirked.

He sighed and started to rise. "Maybe I'll have Officer Leon take over with you."

"No, no, no." I clasped my hands in my lap, resisting the urge to rub them together to keep warm. "It's just been a long evening." I drew a large breath and recalled the moments before we made the grisly discovery. "I was standing near the staircase when the lights went out. Polly was right in front of me, and I grabbed hold of her shoulder to make sure she was okay."

Hamson's expression softened, and a look of genuine concern lit his eyes. "What happened next?"

"We heard a noise, like a clatter, or maybe more like pots and pans banging." I closed my eyes to relive the moment. "Then there was a big thump. That had to be when Mason fell into the dining area."

"That lines up with what others have said." He tapped a few keys on the computer. "Continue."

I cleared my throat. "People were making comments, and it didn't really seem like that big a deal until we all realized the lights weren't coming back on. So, I turned on my phone flashlight and went to Dana, who was standing on the opposite side of the room, nearer to the dining area."

"Why were you going to Dana?"

"I figured she'd know where the fuse box is. Plus, I felt bad for her because someone made a joke about the power company turning off their electricity." I rubbed my hands together to keep them warm. "I guess Mason had a reputation for not paying what he owed people."

A curious look creased Hamson's brow. "That's the first I've heard that tonight."

"Do you think it could be a motive?"

Hamson seared me with his dark gaze. "I'm not sharing information with you…you're sharing information with *me*."

"Considering my track record solving murders, you might want to reconsider." I held back a grin. "Believe me, I already have ideas."

"Such as?"

"I'll tell you, if you'll tell me."

"Not even a fat chance." He pointed at me with his pen. "And if you withhold information, you'll find yourself in a heap of trouble. Those state police are on their way back, and they won't cut you any slack."

I shivered, remembering how by-the-book they were when they were called in to investigate the last murder. "Anyway, just so you know, I didn't see anyone here with blood on their clothing— at least that I could tell with the whole light situation."

Hamson rolled his neck, then pinched the bridge of his nose. "Please stop trying to play junior detective."

"Fine. I was just trying to help. And it stands to reason that whoever did the deed probably has blood spatter on their clothing." I held up one finger as an idea came to me. "You should get one of those black lights they have on TV and shine it all over everyone, just in case they tried to wipe it off."

He ignored my advice and barreled ahead. "I'd like to request you send any photographs, audio, or visual evidence to the department to aid our investigation." He angled the small computer towards me and showed me the address.

"Sure." I pulled out my phone and selected all the pictures I'd taken.

"Thank you for your cooperation, Ms. Crumb."

"Seriously? Are we really back to that?" I pleaded with him over the TV tray.

He leaned in so close I could almost feel his breath. "We are in an investigation." His jaw ticked, and he leaned back, keeping a professional distance. "Now, how about you tell me where your *boyfriend* is."

Chapter Six

AFTER POLLY PUT out the call to the gang, it didn't take long for everyone to convene at my house, despite the late hour. Well, late for those in our group who regularly went to bed by eight. The volume level rose as everyone started talking about Naomi's pending nuptials. But no one was more excited tonight than Cujo.

My little golden fluff ball circled from Aunt Lulu to Verity to Naomi and Polly, begging for attention. When he didn't get it, he started nipping at each person's feet. Unlike Cujo, Pooh Bear sat in the corner and chewed on his squeaky toy while the rest of us gathered in the kitchen.

"I want you all to be my bridesmaids." Naomi pulled a tissue out of her brassiere and wiped her eyes. "I'm just so excited."

"We'll have to have a special planning session." Lulu beamed at Naomi, then turned to Polly and me. "In the meantime, can someone please tell us what's going on? Another murder?"

"Can we get a snack first?" Polly plopped down at the table and rubbed her stomach. "I hate to say it, but all this murder stuff is making me hungry."

I hated to admit she was right, never mind that we ate at the party. "Let me grab some snacks before we give everyone a rundown of what happened." I threw my hair into a messy bun and headed for the pantry while the others chatted.

Though the shelves were nearly empty, I still managed to find crackers, olives, cheese, summer sausage, and dip for a nice little spread on the cutting board. In addition to that, I pulled out some candy and sugary treats I'd been secretly stashing and placed them in a large plastic bowl. Then, I grabbed some napkins, small plates, and toothpicks to pick up the food without touching it.

Verity poked her head inside my fridge. "Don't you have any veggies? Carrot sticks and celery would be great with this." Leave it to her to be my conscience.

"I haven't exactly had time to shop, what with all the murders and whatnot." Sadly, I didn't shop for a lot of vegetables even when there wasn't a murder happening. Something about being in Beaver Bluff caused me to let my guard down, unlike back in LA, where I actually believed carbs would kill me. But I wouldn't worry about that tonight, especially since Griff was bound to work it all off me in the morning at the gym.

As though sensing my insecurities, Aunt Lulu spoke while nibbling on a bleu cheese-filled olive. "That dress looks fabulous on you."

Verity sat at the table and scooped up Cujo, setting him on her lap. "Not to be accusatory, but were you trying to impress James?"

Polly groaned as she grabbed a cracker. "Of course not. Trust me, there were no sparks between them this evening, at least on KC's side. She's just trying to make him miss what he can't have." Once again, Polly and I were on the same wavelength.

"That's right, dear. Stay strong." Naomi patted my hand. "You don't need that no-good scoundrel now that you have Officer Handsome."

Everyone snickered. More than once, I'd accidentally called Hamson the wrong name. Easy mistake. I dragged my cracker through the dip, still second-guessing my lack of veggie intake. "I don't have Hamson, Handsome, or anyone else. That became pretty clear tonight."

Just thinking about the litany of questions Hamson shot at me while we were on the porch caused my heart to palpitate. No matter what I said, he seemed convinced that there was more to James's and my situation than me just trying to get rid of him. And the fact that James was missing didn't help. It was almost like Hamson thought I was covering for James, which I most definitely was not. I wanted to know where he was as much as everyone else.

Aunt Lulu cleared her throat and banged an imaginary gavel on the table to call us to order. "As much as I'd love to sit here gabbing all night, I have to be at the bakery at four in the morning. Can we get the rundown?"

"I want more than a rundown. I want all the juicy details." Naomi dabbed her mouth with a napkin, careful not to smudge her coral lipstick, which was already outside the lines of her lips. If I had to guess, which I really didn't want to, she'd probably come straight over from Walter's house where they had what she liked to call a "smooch fest."

"Me, too. I need deets." Verity cradled Cujo, who looked up and licked her chin.

Lulu sighed, even though we all knew she wouldn't want to get left out of any of it. "Sleep is overrated. Okay, let's hear it."

Polly and I started talking at once until Lulu made us slow down and take turns. Polly went first. "Everyone was having a great time with the music, the laughter, the food. And then the lights went out. A few minutes later, Mason fell out of the kitchen and into the dining room with a stainless steel skewer in his chest."

Naomi's eyes went wide. "A skewer to the heart? It's like that one game—it was so-and-so, in the kitchen, with a skewer."

"The question is, who *is* so-and-so in this case?" Verity asked in a mysterious tone.

Who, indeed, would perpetrate such a gruesome crime? The images of finding Mason on the floor replayed in my head, a crimson stain on his shirt and his cold eyes fixed on the ceiling. A shiver ran through my body, and I drew a long breath to calm myself.

Pooh Bear dropped his squeaky toy and wandered over to me. I ruffled his fur, grateful for his comfort. Truly, I was thankful for all the ladies here. I wasn't ready to be alone, and I had a feeling Polly felt the same, whether she would admit it or not.

"Can you give us more details? I'm having a hard time picturing what happened." Verity continued cuddling Cujo while snacking on a cube of cheese.

"Most everyone was in the front room here. That's where the dancing was, and the people taking pictures together." Polly drew imaginary lines over the table with her hands. "And that area is separated from the dining room by a long island countertop, here. That's where all the food was, including the line for the shish kebab. KC and I were next to that, near the staircase, talking to James." She looked at each of the ladies and lowered her voice. "Before he *disappeared*."

Everyone gasped.

"Hold up." Verity gave Cujo a tiny bit of summer sausage. "James disappeared. Was that before the electricity went out?"

"Yes, shortly before that," I confirmed.

"And now James is gone? Like gone-gone." Verity looked between Polly and me.

"Yes, gone-gone. No one has seen or heard from him since, as far as I know. I think the police are looking for him." My stomach cratered, just thinking about James and where he may have fled to, or more importantly, why. I drew a fortifying breath before my confession. "I actually tried calling him before you all got here, but he didn't answer."

"You called him? *Why?*" Lulu asked. "He's probably a suspect now, for crying out loud."

"First, I wanted to see if he was all right because it's the decent thing to do. But then I wanted to see what he had to say for himself, especially after everyone started accusing him of…" I motioned with my hand, hoping my friends would fill in the blanks for themselves.

"Of…" Lulu, Verity, and Naomi all prodded at once.

"Murdering Mason." Polly shrugged, then she popped a cracker into her mouth. She didn't finish it before speaking again. "Someone said the murderer had to be the guy with the man bun. And there was only one man bun at the party."

"Who said it, and how would they know?" Skepticism tinged Verity's voice.

"I'm not sure anyone knows who said it since it was still dark —except for our phone lights. But once it was out there, everyone ran with it." The moments all blurred together in my mind as I tried to sort through the order of events.

"I still don't understand why everyone would say that." Lulu's brow furrowed, which meant she was deep in thought. "It's not like anyone in town knows him or would have a reason to think he was the killer."

"Whoever said it first probably thinks it's him because James and Mason had an argument before the party." I bit my lip, not wanting to implicate my ex and not sure why I even cared. "Someone must have overheard them."

Lulu leaned forward. "Why on earth were they fighting? They just met. I'll admit, Mason could be a little abrasive—"

"God rest his soul," Naomi added.

"I just don't understand." Lulu shook her head.

"Apparently, Mason made some rude and suggestive comments about me, and James wasn't having it." I recalled the anger in his eyes when he told me about his encounter with the B&B owner.

"So he skewered Mason!" Naomi spoke with conviction.

"No, he most definitely did *not* kill Mason." I knew James was not a great guy by anyone's standards, but I knew equally well that he was not a murderer. He just didn't have it in him.

"So James wasn't with you when the power shut off?" Verity asked.

"Nope," Polly answered before I could. "And like I said, no one has seen him since."

"Where, exactly, was he when the lights went out, then?" Lulu motioned to the table, where Polly had been describing the layout of the scene.

"It's like this." I rearranged the food on the cutting board to create a visual. "Here's where Polly and I were talking to James." I grabbed a few olives to represent Polly and me, and a cheese cube to stand in for James. "Most everyone was in the front room, and a bunch of people formed a conga line." I grabbed some licorice vines to demonstrate as I tried to remember who all was in the line. Then I mentioned talking to Griff, using hard candy for him, as well as Holly and Randall, the jeweler. They, too, had wandered off before the electricity cut out.

"Don't forget about the people taking selfies with the boss." Polly set up some crackers to represent the people lining up for funny photo ops with Benson Michaels. She proceeded to tell the story from her point of view. She relayed our conversation with James and how he crossed the room to go after Mason, who she represented with a slice of summer sausage.

I got up to get a drink and clear my head. Pooh Bear stayed on my heels, as if sensing I needed extra comfort tonight. When I returned to the table, the hard candy was missing. "All right, who ate Griff?"

Naomi swallowed.

"You should have eaten James, because he's also missing in real life." Polly harrumphed and popped cheese-cube James into her mouth. "In any case, that's when the lights went out, and we all heard a giant thump!" She stabbed the hunk of meat that represented Mason with a toothpick and placed it on the part of the cutting board that represented the dining room.

I would never eat summer sausage again.

"That's it—James did it." Naomi crossed her arms over her bosom. "There's no other reason he'd be on the lam."

"He's not on the lam," I argued, even though I couldn't find a plausible reason for him to be missing. "Trust me. He didn't kill Mason." I ate an olive that was either me or Polly.

Lulu looked at me and exhaled. "I can appreciate you wanting to think the best of people, but how can you be so sure?"

I paused, sifting through my conflicting emotions. Not that I wanted to think the best of James—I wasn't actually that nice—it was more…I struggled to put my finger on it. "He's just not the type. He can't even watch scary movies." I thought back to our time together, realizing how delicate James's sensibilities were compared to other people I knew. "*If* he were going to kill someone, which I don't think he could, he'd do something less…messy. Like, use poison."

Verity nodded. "Yeah, that makes sense. He does come off a little squeamish."

"I've only seen him a few times, but I can see what you're saying. He definitely gives off that vibe," Naomi agreed.

Polly snorted and shook her head. "Remember the old days when a man could just be a man and *pop* someone?"

"Polly!" we all cried in unison.

"What?" She shrugged. "You know it's true."

"I don't know any such thing, and you can't say things like that. It's just not *right*," Lulu said. Then a cacophony broke out as everyone debated Polly's statement. Pooh Bear lifted his head off my lap and added his two cents with a few loud barks.

Then he hustled into the living room and started growling. Cujo jumped off Verity's lap and followed, chiming in with his tiny yips. We all stopped talking and watched my pups jump around with nervous energy.

Suddenly, the doorbell rang.

Chapter Seven

I TUGGED open the front door. "James!"

"Shh." He threw a glance over his shoulder and hunched further into his hoodie. "Let me in."

Pooh Bear leaped at James, and I pulled my pooch back before he could do damage. Clearly, Pooh had great instincts, but that didn't mean I wanted him to shred James to bits. At least not before we could find out what happened.

I opened the door wider to let in my unexpected guest, along with a cold gust of wind. James guarded his messenger bag as he scuttled past a snarling Pooh Bear and a yipping Cujo. He stopped short when he saw the ladies gathered at the table, who all stared at him agog. I pushed against the unwieldy door to close it tightly.

"Didn't realize you had company." James glanced from me to the gang as he pulled the hoodie off his head.

"Yeah, it's not like all the cars out front were a dead giveaway or anything." Polly chortled, then spoke behind her hand toward the other ladies. "Not the sharpest crayon in the box."

The others muttered in agreement.

"Look, I know I'm not a fan favorite around here, but I don't have anywhere else to go." James shrugged off his messenger bag and his coat, leaving them both on the couch. "The B&B is off-limits, and there aren't any available rooms in town."

I fisted my hands on my waist. "Where have you been? Have you talked to the police?"

The ladies chimed in with questions, too, causing the dogs to croon. James's gaze widened as he looked between the gals at the kitchen table and me, stupefied. He dropped onto the couch, as though sapped of all his energy. "Sorry, I'm a little shaken up, and I just need to sit for a minute and think."

"Boy, he really *doesn't* have a strong constitution, just like you said." Naomi tsked.

"You told them that?" James spoke with a wobbly voice and hurt in his eyes.

"Believe it or not, I was defending you." I shrugged, then set my phone on the end table as I sat on the rocker. The gang dragged their chairs into the living room. "First, do the police know where you are?"

A meek expression crossed James's face as he offered a slight shake of his head. His man bun slid down a notch.

"Have you talked to them at all?" I pressed.

He bit his lip and seemed to shrink into himself when he shook his head again.

Everyone groaned in unison, then Polly aimed a comment at me. "You'd better get him out of here. They could haul you in for aiding and abetting."

Naomi covered her mouth. "In that case, he needs to leave right now."

"I don't think it works that way," Verity offered. "Unless he's been formally charged, I don't think the police can do anything to KC."

"That doesn't mean she should harbor a criminal." Aunt Lulu folded her arms, shooting James a death glare. "You need to tell us exactly what you know and what you did to Mason."

"I didn't do anything." James palmed his chest, and as much as I hated to defend him, I knew he was telling the truth.

"Then why'd you disappear?" Polly flicked a challenging expression at him. "Everyone was looking for you."

"That's exactly why I left. Everyone was throwing around accusations, and I didn't know what else to do." He scratched his head, causing wisps to escape and fall around his face.

We all started talking at once, telling him the worst thing he could do was flee the scene. Pooh Bear chimed in with a few sharp barks to emphasize the point.

Aunt Lulu shushed us. "Let's all calm down and give James a chance to tell us what happened."

James leaned forward and rested his elbows on his knees. "When I was talking to KC and Polly before the lights went out, I noticed Mason giving KC the eye. I mean, it was just wrong the way he was leering at you, like he wanted to take you and—"

"Yes, we get the picture." I shuddered, remembering how Mason had turned unexpectedly wolfish.

"So, I left you and Polly to go after Mason. There was no way I was going to let that dude get away with the things he'd said earlier in the day and the way he was creeping on you at the party." He looked at me with anticipation, as though I was going to fall at his feet with gratitude.

Instead, I leaned over and picked up Cujo and cradled him to my chest. "Go on."

The room had quieted, and the ladies edged forward in their seats, eyes wide. Even I couldn't wait to hear what happened next.

"I made my way through the crowd, and Mason saw me coming. He turned around and went through the dining area, toward the kitchen." James made a turning motion to illustrate his point. Clearly, he enjoyed everyone's rapt attention. His tone smoothed out as he shifted into storytelling mode, casting himself as the hero. "Mason probably thought I wouldn't follow him into the kitchen, but I did. I had to make sure he left KC alone."

Polly's eyes slivered. "So, you were with him when the lights went out?"

"Not exactly. Inside the kitchen, Mason turned around really fast. We were toe-to-toe, staring each other down, ready to fight." He fisted his hands and made a boxing motion. "I told him to quit creeping on KC and to *back off*." He practically spat the last two words.

Everyone gasped.

"Then he told me to get out, or he'd call the police." James held his hands up in a surrender position. "I don't need that kind of bad press, so I was like dude, just heed the warning. Then he said I had to get out of the B&B by morning and that I had to quit eating their guest's food." There was a slight mimic to his tone, and I could mentally hear Mason say the words.

Polly flashed him a dubious expression. "Wait, I don't recall seeing you come back out of the kitchen."

To be fair, she wouldn't have noticed him because she was paying attention to me and to the cream puffs we were nipping. That was around the same time I'd decided I didn't need a new client that badly, and we were going to leave.

James met Polly's gaze. "I didn't come back that way. Mason pointed at a hallway off to the side of the kitchen. I guess so I wouldn't go through the front and eat any more of the catered food."

"Did you take off out a back door?" Verity eyed the kitchen table, and I was almost afraid she'd make James diagram his exit with whatever olives and crackers we had left. "Does that mean you were outside when it all happened?"

James shook his head, his man bun taking another slide. "No. The side door led to a storage area and a laundry room. There's a staircase back there that goes to the second floor where my room is…was."

Lulu nodded thoughtfully. "I believe many homes from that era had back staircases for servants to use."

James continued. "Yeah, it was narrow and dark—I didn't realize at that moment it was dark because the electricity cut out. But when I got to the second floor, I couldn't see a thing, and there was no music."

"We were all wondering what was going on at that point," Polly interjected.

"I wanted to see what all the ruckus was, so I found my way to the main staircase and stood at the top." James's expression changed. "That's about the time KC turned on her phone light, and we all saw…" His mouth pinched, and he clutched his stomach in a dry heave.

"Buck up." Polly waved him off. "Considering what happened to him, Mason didn't look all that bad."

The rest of us looked at her, speechless.

She rolled her eyes. "What? I was a military nurse. You see stuff."

Well, that explained a few things. I made a mental note to ask Polly more about her working life, as it seemed like the whole time I'd known her, she'd been retired. I stroked Cujo's golden fur and rocked him gently while he slept. Just holding my little guy took my blood pressure down a few notches. I needed to stay calm as I considered what to do next. There was no way I could keep James here without alerting the police.

James shuddered and visibly shook his arms as though discarding memories from this evening. "Anyway, I heard someone in the crowd accuse *me* of killing that dude." He palmed his chest, his face awash in disbelief. "It must've been someone who overheard us fighting earlier today. But even though I thought the guy was scum, I could never do *that*."

"I've got to say, I'm almost inclined to believe him." Naomi nibbled a cracker.

Murmurs of agreement rose in the living room. Even though James was my nemesis, in this, I had to concur. He was innocent —but that meant it was more important than ever that he talk to the police.

I shifted in my seat, careful not to wake Cujo. "I'm guessing that's when you left the B&B?"

James nodded. "I backed down the hallway far enough so no one could see me and grabbed my bag inside my room. It was easy enough to use the back staircase and leave through the door off of the storage room."

"Let me ask you this," I said as I surreptitiously slid my phone from the end table to my side, away from James. "Did you see anyone in the kitchen when you followed Mason in? I mean, there had to be others in there. If you didn't kill Mason, whoever was in the kitchen would be the one with the best opportunity." I started casually swiping a message on my phone. If this text didn't make Hamson believe I wasn't taking up with James again, nothing would. I hit send.

James shrugged, palms up. "I was so focused on Mason, I didn't notice if there was anyone else."

"Just like he didn't notice our cars out front," Verity pointed out.

"That's kind of a crucial bit of information." Lulu frowned. "Think hard. You were probably the last person to see Mason alive, other than the killer. Did he seem nervous or scared? Was he aware of anyone else besides you? Think back on all the details from the moment you went inside the kitchen."

The others agreed, and Polly spoke up. "You might have some detail, no matter how small, that points to the killer."

"Dude, that's a lot of pressure." James blew out a long breath that sent wisps of his hair aflutter. "I need to calm down. I drove around for a while and spent some time at the water." He glanced between us ladies. "Do you have any idea how cold the ocean is here? Anyway, I just wanted to lie low and collect my thoughts. Maybe tonight I could stay here—"

"No!" we all shouted in unison. Pooh Bear barked, and Cujo stirred against my chest, not too pleased with the disruption.

James held his hands up like he was at gunpoint.

For the next few minutes, we continued to badger James with questions he was unable to answer. If he couldn't handle us, I wasn't sure how he could handle the Beaver Bluff PD.

Then the doorbell rang.

I smiled as I rose. "Let me just get that." Through the peephole I saw my real knight in shining armor, even if he didn't know it yet. I set Cujo on the ground next to Pooh and tugged open the door. "Officer Hamson," I said, careful to enunciate his name. "What a surprise."

Hamson's dark eyes narrowed. "But you're the one who texted me." He peered around me, trying to see inside. "How did you get my number, anyway?"

"You'd be surprised what one can find online," I said. Verity had taught me that. I stood aside to let him in. "There's someone here you should talk to."

James groaned. "Dude, I wasn't ready yet."

"For once, this isn't about you," I said in a sing-song voice. "Officer, take him away." I whisked my arm toward the street.

"That's not how this works," Hamson spoke under his breath. He cleared his throat, then turned to James. "I presume you're the gentleman who went missing from the party?"

"Yeah, that would be me."

"I'd like to ask you a few questions." Hamson's face remained stoic. "We could do it here or at the station."

James rose and slung his messenger bag over his shoulder. "I think my chances are better at the station."

"You can follow me in your car. It shouldn't take long." Hamson stood aside to make room for James.

"Thanks a lot, KC." James sighed as he brushed past me and walked into the night.

I leaned close to Hamson and inhaled the faint scent of cologne and a hard night's work. "Shouldn't you make him ride in the cruiser?" I whispered.

"Again, that's not how this works." Hamson squinched his eyes at me.

"Well, at least now you know I wasn't hiding anything, and I'm most definitely not with James." I locked eyes with Hamson, willing him to remember just days ago when he revealed he had feelings for me.

Hamson scrubbed his five o'clock shadow and exited the house. "We'll talk later."

"I'm holding you to that," I called after him as he strode down the walkway. I turned on the porch light just so I could see him a little longer on this moonless night.

Hamson paused and glanced over his shoulder. He teased me with the faintest hint of a smile. "That's not how this works."

I grinned as I shut the door. I knew I could get to him, and it was only a matter of time before we could pick up where we left off.

All at once, everyone started in with noisy chatter, positing theories, conclusions, and commentary. Once the room quieted, Polly looked at me and spoke. "I'll say one thing for James—his messy bun looks as good as yours."

Chapter Eight

IF THERE WAS one thing I hated more than getting out of bed when it was still dark, it was kettlebells. Or treadmills. Actually, any type of exercise equipment that made me hurt.

Griff counted down to the end of the set, then he clapped his hands, eliciting the attention of the other early morning gymgoers. "Good job, KC. Your hard work's going to pay off."

Really? Because it didn't feel like it every time I slid into my clothes that had mysteriously shrunk a little more each time I wore them. All the pastries at Crumb's hadn't helped, and neither had the extra puffs last night at the B&B.

"That was some party, wasn't it?" Griff asked as though reading my thoughts.

I set the kettlebell down and wiped the sweat out of my eyes. "Just curious…why were you and Holly there?" I panted between words. "I thought it was a party exclusively for that law firm."

Griff shrugged his massive shoulder. "I do some maintenance and carpentry work for Benson Michaels now and then at his office. We go way back." He preened in the mirror, pretending not to notice the women at the leg press machines checking him out.

"I saw that you and Holly were one of the first people to talk to the police. Polly and I weren't so lucky. We were some of the last." I unscrewed the cap on my water bottle and took a swig.

"You might want to stretch." He motioned for me to copy him as he continued our conversation in the mirror. "The police were pretty quick with us. I didn't have a lot to say."

"Didn't you see anything?"

"Did anyone? It was dark. Plus, Holly and me didn't have any pictures to show the police, so they let us go." Griff rolled his neck in time to the music playing from the speakers overhead.

I followed his lead. "Since you go way back with the Michaels people, do you know anyone who wanted to kill Mason?"

Griff stopped stretching and dropped his beefy arms to his sides. "Wait a sec…are you doing that thing again?"

"What thing?"

"Where you ask questions and poke around?"

"You mean investigating?"

Griff nodded, and his eyes narrowed. Weights clinked in the background. "Isn't that how you got hurt last time?"

By "last time," he meant what still felt like mere days ago when someone conked me on the head after I left the gym. I made a mental note to pay attention to my surroundings when I went out to my car this morning. Staying alert was part of the basic self-defense work I'd been doing with Verity.

"Actually, I'm not trying to do anything." Except trying to speed things along so James could leave town. "I'm just curious, is all." I continued stretching, and this time, Griff copied me.

"You know what they say about curiosity." He stretched his quads with perfect balance while holding his ankle to his backside. "But to answer your question, no, I don't know anyone who wanted to kill Mason. I didn't even know him, but not too many people did from what I heard last night after it all went down. Guy kept to himself."

Except for when he didn't, like when he leered at me. I shuddered at the memory of his roving eyes and bristly walrus mustache. I matched Griff's stance but had to hop a few times to catch my balance. "Were you in the conga line when the lights went out?" Last night when we recreated the scene back at my house, I'd placed Griff on the opposite side of the room as Polly and me, but I wasn't altogether sure.

"No, Holly and I were chatting with one of her clients who works for Benson Michaels. We were kind of near the backdrop where everyone was taking pictures."

Just as I'd thought. I stopped stretching. "And from where you were, who did you see close to the kitchen? It had to be someone who could get there quickly when the lights went out."

Griff lowered his leg to the floor and frowned thoughtfully. "You're assuming it was someone taking advantage of the sudden darkness. Maybe…" He smiled at himself in the mirror. "Just maybe, whoever killed that guy cut the lights on purpose."

That was, perhaps, the most intelligent thing I'd ever heard from Griff. He sent my mind spinning in new directions. I mentally scrambled for a thread to pull from my tired brain, one that would give me a place to start.

Not that I was investigating.

Griff pulled his arms over his head and groaned with a final stretch. "Anyway, I think we all know who did it."

"We do?"

"Yeah, everyone who was at the party pretty much agrees. It was that guy you were talking to." He motioned to the top of his head. "The one with the man bun."

"No, no, no. It was definitely not him."

"How do you know?"

"Because I *know* him." I willed Griff not to ask any further questions.

"How do you know him?"

I winced as I uncapped my water bottle. "He's my ex-boyfriend. I'm telling you, he didn't do it."

Griff raised a questioning brow, his mouth tilted in a smirk. "Let me ask you this—why is he your ex?"

"Because he…sort of cheated. I guess." My words faded, covered by the music in the background.

He poised his finger to his mouth. "Mmm-hmm. And did you ever think he would do that?"

"No, of course not." I was quick to answer.

Griff nodded, as if already agreeing with himself over what he was about to say. He cuffed my shoulder with his meaty paw. "I'm sorry to be the one to tell you, Cupcake, but people don't always turn out to be who you think they are."

And he should know, after what he and his fiancée Holly had been through, but I held back from saying so. Instead, I paused to consider what he said. Aside from Griff's Cupcake comment—which bothered me considerably less now that I'd gotten to know him—his words threw the tiniest speck of doubt into my heart.

<hr>

AFTER WORKING OUT, I raced home to take a quick shower and pick up my boys before heading to Crumb's. Polly was already at the bakery to greet us at the back door, where she took Pooh Bear's leash and cradled Cujo against her chest. Her eyes softened, and I had a feeling that taking the pooches to the park while I worked was one of the best parts of her day.

Inside, I took a moment to bask in the vanilla-scented air before donning a frilly pink Have a Crumby Day apron. "Good morning, Aunt Lulu." I hobbled over to the industrial-sized mixer and kissed her cheek.

"Tough workout?" she asked over the whirr.

"Always. But with the way you keep feeding me, I need it."

She rolled her eyes at my comment. Then she turned off the mixer and lowered her voice, presumably so her assistant, Bert, wouldn't listen in. "Have you heard anything since last night?"

"No, but I had a chat with Griff. I have a few ideas." I winked.

"Hold on, now." She fisted her hands on her hips. "You need to stay out of it this time. I mean it."

"Then why were you asking if I'd heard anything?"

She hesitated. "Just curious."

Apparently, curiosity ran in the family. Be that as it may, I wasn't interested in investigating, especially after being injured last time. If I happened to come up with a tip or two to point the police in the right direction, that was just me being a good citizen. It was practically my civic duty.

Out front, 80s music played from the speakers, and even though it wasn't yet eight o'clock, a queue of people snaked toward the door. Hopefully, the social media campaigns I'd launched since coming back to Beaver Bluff were at least partially responsible for the uptick in business.

I slid into place at the counter next to Krystal. She worked the line, pouring drinks and slinging pastries and bagels like a pro. I took orders, made more coffee, and shifted the contents of the display cases when the items sold down. Though Krystal and I had had a rocky start when I moved here—mostly because I'd thought she or her husband might be a murderer—we'd learned to work companionably.

Customers came and went for the next few hours, and the bakery was abuzz with talk of the murder. At least half a dozen people asked me what I'd seen and who I thought was guilty. Apparently, the Beaver Bluff grapevine was alive and well.

Around ten o'clock, people stopped trickling through the door, and I was finally able to shift my attention to other tasks. Tasks which I found infinitely more satisfying. I started by taking pastry photos and scheduling posts with strategic hashtags. Then I responded to follower comments on social media and checked numbers on the small ad campaigns I'd launched last week.

Coffee in hand, I sat at an empty table near the window with my tablet and took a moment to soak in the ocean view across the street. It was nice to relax after being on the go all morning. Hopefully, Aunt Lulu would hire someone to take my place at Crumb's soon, then I could focus on growing my own business. In the meantime, helping at Crumb's had its benefits, like the pumpkin scone I was about to devour.

"Oh good, you're here." James hovered over me, his shadow

looming. I hadn't even seen him come in.

My heart sank a little as I acknowledged him with a weak smile. For a few blissful moments, I'd forgotten all about James and murder and the trouble surrounding us. I closed the cover on my tablet and looked up at my disheveled ex. "Rough night?"

His mouth puckered. "Very funny."

"It wasn't meant to be." I popped the rest of the scone into my mouth and savored the hint of cinnamon and the crumbly texture. Delicious, even without clotted cream or jam.

"Do you have any idea what I'm going through right now?" He dropped onto the seat across from me and raked his hand through his hair, which he wore loose today. Probably because everyone in town was on the lookout for the guy with the man bun.

"You brought it on yourself. You should've just stayed in LA, then none of this would be happening." I casually sipped my coffee, feigning less interest than I felt. In truth, I had a smidgen of sympathy for him, but if I let James know that, he'd exploit it and try to wiggle back into my life.

Outside, Polly waved to me as she and the pooches paused at the bench. Naomi, whose puffy white hair billowed in the ocean breeze, joined her. They both made faces behind James's back, indicating they felt sorry for me being stuck with him. At least that's how I interpreted them.

James scrubbed his face with his hands. "The police told me not to leave town."

"You know they can't really do that, right? Unless you're under arrest, they can't legally mandate whether or not you can leave." I spoke with confidence, even though I wasn't one-hundred percent sure.

James caught my eye. "If I leave now, there will always be a cloud of doubt. People will think I skipped town because I'm guilty, which I'm not."

"Excuse me." A lady at the table next to us waved her napkin at me. "I'm not trying to listen in, but why don't you just solve this murder like you did the last ones? I heard all about that."

I motioned for her to turn back around. She harrumphed but complied.

James's face scrunched. "You solved murders?"

"Never mind about that."

Polly breezed inside Crumb's, matting down her windblown hair as she approached us. "Are you almost done with your tête-à-tête? Naomi and I want to grab a little lunch."

"Yeah, I think we're about finished." I started to rise, but James clamped his hand over my wrist.

"Wait. With the B&B closed off, I don't have any place to stay. And like I said, I'm not supposed to leave. What should I do?" His eyes pleaded, softening my heart by a fraction.

I groaned. "I don't know. Are you sure there's no other places open?"

"Your little village here only has two motels."

"Village?" Polly folded her arms and pursed her lips at James.

"You know what I mean. Anyway, there aren't any rooms." He lowered his voice. "I spent last night in my car." That explained his haggard appearance.

"What, exactly, are you wanting me to do? I can't magically make a room appear." I slid my hand out from under his.

"Can I stay at your place? Just until a room opens up, maybe at the end of the weekend or something." He attempted to muster his million-watt smile, but even that seemed a bit beyond his reach.

"No, you can't stay with me. It's not proper or right." On that point, I refused to budge. Besides, if I let James stay, however innocently, Hamson would never believe I had no interest in my ex. I took another sip of coffee and savored the cream. "Look, you only have to tough it out for—"

"Come on, it's not that big a deal—"

"There's no way. My house isn't big enough for the both of us."

"It's just a few——"

"Hey, hey, hey. Enough." Polly held her hands up, then looked at me. "He only needs a place to be until something opens up, right?"

I mumbled something not nice under my breath.

Polly tsked me, much as she had when I was a teen. Then she spoke with resolution. "Let James hang out at your place, and you can stay with me."

"Whew," he said, suddenly appearing much less haggard than he had moments before. "And while we're at it, maybe you can help find the real killer."

Apparently, I would not have a moment of peace or be able to get on with my life until I did.

Chapter Nine

THE GREAT THING about bunking with Polly was her home's proximity to the B&B. Though her house was around the corner, her second-story sitting room afforded us a nice view. We could see the state police working the scene, at least with the help of binoculars. Polly had two pairs plus a hand scope—enough for herself, Naomi, and me. I briefly considered asking Polly why she had all the reconnaissance gear, but it was probably better not to know.

The three of us sat on our knees, backwards, on her couch. The pooches meandered around the room, sniffing out new adventures and playing with their toys.

"Whoa, get a load of that." Naomi peered through the binoculars.

I quickly scanned the area, but the investigators had gone back inside. "What are you seeing?" I adjusted the settings on the hand scope to get a better view, even though my left eye hurt from squinting.

"That front garden area. It's gorgeous. Those Red Valerians would look great in my engagement photos." Naomi pulled her eyes away from the binoculars. "Do you think I could book my engagement party there on short notice?"

Polly and I turned to look at our friend. Polly spoke first. "You know we're supposed to be looking for clues, right?"

"Well, *excuse* me for multi-tasking." Naomi sniffed. She was, by far, the most sensitive of us all.

I patted her arm. "I think Dana from the B&B might take a break for a while, considering what happened to her brother. But I'll help you find a venue that's just perfect for you and Walter."

"Thank you. That would be lovely." She patted my back in return.

Pooh Bear hopped onto the couch between Naomi and me. Cujo yipped from the floor, still too small to make the jump. Polly bent over and picked him up, and together we all watched out the window. The dogs' heads moved back and forth in sync with the birds flitting between the trees.

"Look, here comes Antonio!" Polly pointed across the way at Hamson, emerging from the police cruiser. "He's got Officer Leon with him." She pulled the binoculars away from her eyes. "I wonder what they're doing there. Did they work the crime scene for the last murder? I thought just the state police did that."

I hopped off the couch and whistled for my pooches. "I don't know, but I'm going to find out. Keep your eyes peeled for anything I might not see while I'm walking over to the B&B." Together, the dogs and I scampered down the stairs. I grabbed the spare leashes Polly kept on a hook by her front door and got my little guys ready.

The chill outside caught me off guard, but we didn't have time to go back for a coat. Instead, I picked up the pace until Cujo stopped to sniff the weeds sprouting between the cracks in the sidewalk. I tugged, but he wouldn't budge. Pooh Bear released a warning bark to get Cujo moving again.

We quickly rounded the corner, then immediately slowed down when Hamson caught sight of us. He did a double-take, as though not believing it was me.

I offered a full-armed wave. "Hey, there!" My heels clacked on the pavement as we crossed the street. "Fancy meeting you here." I grinned.

Hamson leaned against the cruiser and crossed his legs at the ankle. "Me? I'm *supposed* to be here." He glanced over his shoulder at the forensics team on the porch, then leaned close to me and lowered his voice. "What are *you* doing here?"

I held up the leashes. "Walking the dogs."

Hamson tilted his head and raked me with his dark gaze. "Aren't you a little far from home? I didn't realize you were in the habit of taking five-mile walks in heels."

"Well, that's a little judgy of you." Never mind the throb in my pinky toes.

"And no jacket."

"Awww, look at you, brushing up on your observational skills. Bravo." I golf-clapped, causing Cujo to yip with excitement.

A smile illuminated Hamson's face before he schooled his expression. "C'mon, you know what I mean. What gives? You don't need to get mixed up in all this. Don't forget what happened to you last time." He threw another glance over his shoulder.

I inched closer and inhaled the spicy notes of his aftershave. "Are you concerned about me?" I looked up at him, taking in his dark, tousled hair and the strong planes of his face.

Hamson's lips parted as he leaned in so close I could feel his breath. He paused a beat before he spoke in a low, sultry tone. "I'm concerned about all the citizens of Beaver Bluff."

"Oh, fine." I pulled back to an appropriate distance. "It just so happens that I'm staying at Polly's house around the corner."

"Why are you staying with her? Did something happen?" His eyebrows pinched with concern.

"Yeah—you told James to stay in town, and there's nowhere for him to go except my house." I rubbed my arms against the chilly breeze. "Which means I'm crashing at Polly's. I wouldn't want anyone to get the wrong idea."

Hamson smiled before catching himself and clearing his

throat. "Good to know he heeded the warning and decided to stick around."

"That's because he's not guilty."

"You should leave that to the professionals to decide." Hamson allowed Cujo to sniff his shoe.

"Yeah, yeah, of course." After solving the last two murders in town, some would argue that I, too, was a pro. "So…are you working the scene?" I noted the state police in their gear.

"Not really. Officer Leon and I turned over the witness statements and everything we had last night to the staties." Hamson scanned the area. "We just stopped by to check in with a little new evid—" He cut himself off, and his expression turned stoic once again.

I lowered my voice. "What kind of evidence? Does it have anything to do with who turned the lights off? At first, I thought that someone took advantage of the electricity cutting out, but on second thought…" I leaned in and spoke conspiratorially. "I believe someone cut the lights on purpose."

"Why do you think that?"

"When I was here two days ago, there was some construction guy, or maybe he was an electrician. Dana happened to mention that they were having electrical problems." I turned and leaned against the police cruiser, allowing my arm to brush against his. "That's the guy we should be talking to."

"We?" Hamson's eyebrows shot skyward. "There's no we in this."

I folded my arms, careful not to tangle the leashes. "Well, maybe there should be. You might find the killer more quickly."

"It's only day two, and we're already wrapping things up here." He cocked an easy grin. "Tell me this…was the electrician at the party?"

"Er…maybe?" I made a mental note to go over my pictures more closely.

"That's not how we run investigations. We work with facts and evidence." Hamson pushed his body away from the cruiser as

Officer Leon approached with a dubious expression. Then he slid on his sunglasses and opened the driver's side door. "As I said, Ms. Crumb, leave it to the professionals."

———

"LEAVE IT TO THE PROFESSIONALS," I mimicked as I throat-chopped the dummy inside the martial arts studio.

Despite the fact that my body still ached from the early-morning workout with Griff, I couldn't pass up the opportunity to hang out with Verity when she invited me for a little round of self-defense action.

"Honestly, it's like he already forgot who solved the last two murders. It wasn't the local police." I kicked the dummy in the knee. "It wasn't the state police." I poked the dummy in the eyes. "And it certainly wasn't *him*." I grabbed the dummy by the shoulders and kneed it in the groin.

"All right, I think this guy's had enough for one night." Verity cuffed my arms and guided me away from the mannequin. "Are you upset because Hamson didn't have confidence in you or because he was right?" She grabbed her gear and motioned for me to follow her.

I wiped the sweat off my forehead, then picked up my gym bag and slung the strap over my shoulder. "He *may* have made a point. I didn't think about whether or not the contractor or electrician, whatever he is, was at the party. I just hated sounding dumb in front of him and Officer Leon."

"I'm sure no one thought you were dumb." Verity switched off the lights of the studio we'd been training in.

"Officer Leon smirked, for what it's worth." I tightened my messy bun. "I want to be taken seriously because I'm telling you, I have good ideas."

We wandered past a class of kids and teens, their "hi-yas" sounding through the glass. The stench of sweat and hard work filled the air. The evening light shone through the window that faced the town square, signaling an end to the day.

"To be fair, you're not on the Beaver Bluff Police Force, and *they're* not even on the case. There's no reason they should be bouncing ideas with you." She sat on a bench that lined the wall. "That's what I'm here for. Tell me everything that's happened that I don't already know about."

"Well, the latest thing is the investigators are done with the scene. At least it looked that way when I was leaving. But they kept mum about any evidence they'd found." If only they'd spoken a little louder, so I could eavesdrop. I reached inside my bag for my water bottle. I'd filled it with diet soda, but that was my secret.

"Are you going to track down the contractor? Wait, is he a contractor or electrician?" Verity whipped out her phone, presumably to start researching. To her credit, she was the Queen of Research.

"Does someone need a contractor?" The owner of the dojo, who bore a striking resemblance to William Shatner, appeared from his office down the hall. He adjusted the belt on his gi. "I know a contractor."

"I think we've got it, but thanks." Verity smiled at the older gentleman who'd been kind enough to give us free studio time. One day, I would remember his name.

"There's Donovans, Jed Parker, Wally." Faux-William started counting off contractors on his fingers.

"Thanks." I toasted him with my water bottle of soda. "I know who to come to if I need a recommendation."

"Always happy to help." Faux-William nodded at us before disappearing back down the hallway to his office.

I turned to Verity. "I can't remember if Dana called him an electrician or a contractor, but I distinctly remember that when the lights cut out during the party, she said they'd been having electrical problems." I sat next to her on the bench. "Griff mentioned it may not have been a crime of opportunity, but that someone cut the power on purpose."

"That actually seems more likely. That narrows it down to people who know where the fuse box is."

"Not that someone couldn't find that out."

"True," Verity conceded. "But unlikely. It might be best to focus on likely suspects first."

"I guess I'd need to talk to Dana to get a better feel for that. I think she has one employee and…oh!" I gasped, remembering an important detail. I sat taller, then whispered frantically. "When I was hooking up the sound system, I overheard the caterer talking to someone else who said that Mason would get what's coming to him."

"Who was it?"

"I never saw the person. I just overheard from my spot on the floor."

"That's going to be a problem unless Dana knows everyone who was coming and going from her B&B yesterday." Verity bit her lip.

The door opened, and two guys in street clothes walked in, paused, and looked around.

Suddenly, Faux-William appeared again. "May I help you?" Then he began chatting with the guys, who were interested in lessons.

"How does he keep appearing? It's creepy, like he has a sixth sense," I whispered to Verity while glancing at the owner.

"It's not a sixth sense." Verity scooped her hair into a ponytail. "He has cameras all over." She motioned to a black orb that dangled from the ceiling.

"That's right," the owner cut in and spoke to me. "I saw you pummeling my mannequin in studio C. Good job!" He raised his fist high.

I matched his fist with one of my own. "Thanks!" Then it hit me. I turned to my friend, enthusiasm coursing through my veins. "He just gave me an idea. I totally forgot that the B&B has cameras. I'm going to go ask Dana to show me the footage from yesterday afternoon. Maybe she'll recognize the voice."

Verity grimaced at me. "You can't just waltz in after her brother was murdered and ask to see video footage."

"No," I said, rising from the bench. "But I *can* waltz in to grab the rented sound system that I still need to return."

Chapter Ten

AGAINST HER BETTER JUDGMENT, Verity went with me to the B&B.

As soon as we opened the gate and entered the front yard, the sun sank below the ocean's horizon, casting us in shadows. The patio heaters still stood in place from last night, and bits of debris littered the garden. The party-goers-cum-witnesses had not been tidy. Either that or the investigators had shown little regard for the people left behind to clean up.

"Oh, this looks like a nice home. I mean, if not for the murder and the trash." Verity motioned to the plastic champagne flutes in the bushes.

"It is. Naomi wants her engagement party here, but I told her we'd have to find something else." I glanced around, suddenly sorry for the grieving sister stuck with such a mess. "I can't imagine the B&B will be hosting another event anytime soon."

We ascended the porch steps, and I rapped on the door and waited. There was no answer. "Maybe she's not here."

"Or she didn't hear you in this ginormous house." Verity knocked sharply. "Hello? Is anyone home?"

Seconds later, the door creaked open. Dana stood in the entry, half-moons hanging under her eyes and her hair in a stringy braid down her back. "Can I help you?"

"It's just me, and this is my friend Verity. We're sorry for your loss." I inched forward, hoping she'd invite us inside.

Dana opened the door just wide enough for us to enter. "As you can see, it's quite the mess." She led us further into the dimly lit house.

Detritus from the party littered the front room and dining area. The shish kebab fixings, appetizers, and desserts remained on the table, cold and limp. Half-full cups lay abandoned on the standing tables, and the photo backdrop dangled from the wall, holding on by a single corner. Worse, fingerprint powder covered the dining area, and I could only imagine how much powder was in the kitchen.

"Will your workers be by later to help you clean up?" Verity's eyes traveled the room.

Dana slumped against the staircase banister. "What workers? The one I had quit on me. She said she was too freaked out to be here anymore."

"Do you have family in the area you can stay with?" I asked. There was no way she should stay here, surrounded by reminders of the tragedy.

"No. Mason is…was my only family." Her mouth turned down a fraction, but she forged ahead before I could respond. "Why are you here?"

"Why are we here? Because…" *We wanted to ask you for video footage that you may or may not still have that could lead us to your brother's killer.* "I figured I'd better return the sound system. It was supposed to be back earlier today."

Dana drew her cardigan more tightly around her body. "I'm glad you thought of it. I guess that's one more expense to add to this whole fiasco."

I waved off her comment. "Don't worry about it. I've got it covered." It was the least I could do, considering what she had to deal with.

"Go ahead and take what you need. I'll just be upstairs." Dana turned to leave.

"Wait," Verity said.

Dana turned back around. "Is there anything else?"

Verity glanced at me before continuing. "Who's going to help you clean all this up?" Concern pinched her brow, and I knew what she was thinking. But because I'm not as nice as Verity, all I could do was hope that Dana had hired a cleaning crew. Otherwise, I knew what the rest of my night would look like.

Dana offered a humorless laugh. "Your guess is as good as mine." Once again, she turned to leave.

Verity spoke. "Would you like—"

I shot her an elbow and a grimace.

"Some help?" Verity scowled at me in return, then quickly smiled as Dana spun back around.

"That would be amazing." She clutched her chest and offered a faint smile.

Suddenly, I felt a little sheepish about having resisted. Since Polly had the dogs, staying for a few hours to help Dana wouldn't be that hard. "Point us to the garbage bags, and we'll get started."

TWENTY MINUTES INTO THE CLEANUP, we still hadn't sussed out any new information from Dana. Mostly because she excused herself to her office while Verity and I did the dirty work. Thankfully, almost everything was disposable or belonged to the caterer.

"That's someone else we should talk to." I tipped the standing table on its side and folded the legs.

"Who?" Verity swiped a strand of her red hair off her forehead.

I bit my lip, suddenly mindful of the camera watching from the ceiling. "Er…the hairdresser…to fix this mess." I motioned to the inexpertly colored stripes in my hair.

"Okaaaay." The dubious expression on Verity's face made me

feel a little guilty for the tiny lie. But I truly needed a color correction once we finished dealing with the whole murder situation.

"I wonder when the caterer is coming by to get her stuff?" I asked, thinking back to my idea to talk to Carla. She'd been pretty upset with Mason before the party because he hadn't paid what he owed. Not that I suspected her of the murder. After all, a dead Mason was a lot less likely to pay than a live one.

Although, the person who was with her might've had a bone to pick with Mason, too. I hadn't thought to tell Hamson about it last night when he interviewed me. Although, to be fair, he hadn't asked me about anything that happened prior to the lights going out.

"Maybe the caterer doesn't know the scene has been released by the police yet," Verity said.

"Good point. I'll get her number from Dana in a minute and call her." Better yet, it was a great excuse to bring up what I'd overheard and ask if there was video footage. But first, I wanted to see the kitchen. I motioned for Verity to follow me.

I stopped short of the swinging door, where the bloodstain had soaked into the floor. My stomach curdled as memories from last night seeped into my mind. The sound of the door swinging open and the thump of Mason hitting the floor. The unease of the crowd. The sight of his body when I turned on my phone light.

Verity made a gurgling noise behind me. "The death spot."

I grimaced. We'd dealt with death spots before—one being in my own garage—but it never got any easier. I steeled my nerves as I gave a wide berth to the stain in order to get to the kitchen. Dana would have to get an actual biohazard team to get rid of the blood. This was above my pay grade.

We walked through the swinging door and flicked on the lights. Fingerprint powder everywhere, including my fingers. Poor Dana, having had to face this disaster alone—at least before we got here.

"This is worse than I thought." Verity toured the kitchen, and I followed in her wake.

"I think we've gotten ourselves in over our heads, as far as cleaning goes." My eyes roved the room, and I noted the absence of a back door. I eased past the island and the cabinetry, heading towards the storage room that James had described. A metal box was mounted on the wall in a short hallway between the kitchen and a storage area. "Look, here's the breaker switches."

"So, according to his own story, James would have been right here." Verity's eyes went wide. "And yet he says he didn't see anyone. Because if the killer turned off the lights on purpose, they would have had to be right here around the same time. Like, at exactly the same time."

"I know what you're thinking." I kept my voice low as I glanced around for another camera. The last thing I wanted was to talk about the murder and be overheard by Dana.

Verity grabbed my shoulder and forced me to meet her gaze. "Are you sure about James? I mean, it may have been an accident. And he's certainly acting strangely since the murder."

"Skewering someone is not an accident. Anyway, how would you know whether he's acting strangely? You barely met him." Defensiveness rose inside me for reasons I couldn't identify.

"Because he showed up in town, Mr. Laid Back, Cool-As-a-Cucumber. And now he's skittish and on edge."

"That's because he's freaked out like any normal person would be after this experience." I shook off her hand. "Let's get busy. While you start in here, I'll casually talk to Dana."

"Wait, why am I the one cleaning and not—" Her voice cut out as I left the kitchen.

I made the trek through the dining area and front room, then down the short hall leading to the turret office. "Knock, knock." I tapped on the door frame.

Dana startled, then looked up. She sat behind her desk, staring at a laptop screen. "Sorry, I didn't hear you coming."

"I hope you don't mind. I just have a few questions."

"You and everybody else." She leaned back in her squeaky chair and rubbed her forehead.

"Have the police been back by?" I leaned against a small credenza by the window. "Have they shared any theories with you yet?"

"Aside from destroying my home, they haven't done a thing." Dana's chippy voice sent shivers down my spine. She had apparently skipped to the anger part of the grief process.

"Working with them can be…frustrating." I picked up a stray pencil and twirled it, trying to appear more casual than I felt. "I imagine you're exhausted. Did you stay with family last night?"

"As I said, I don't have any other family."

I winced. "Sorry, you did say that. Do you have someplace to stay tonight?"

"Yes." Dana offered no further information. "Any other questions?"

"Actually, I was wondering about your camera." I motioned to the small monitor on her desk.

"What about it?"

I drew a deep breath. "Have you already turned over all the video footage from last night to the police?"

Wariness tinged Dana's eyes. "Well, it so happens that the video cut out with the electricity. There's a large gap during the time my brother…" She brought her fist to her mouth. Then her shoulders heaved with a large breath. "In any case, I sent the video clips to the police from the beginning of the party for all the good it will do. Why do you ask?"

I softened my voice. "Before the party started, I may have overheard something relevant."

"Did you tell the police?"

"I'd forgotten about it until a bit ago, and I thought this might help." I pointed at the monitor. "Someone was talking to the caterer before the party, and they sounded really mad at your brother."

She sat taller. "Who was it?"

"I didn't see them, but I was hoping we could pull up the video. Maybe you'll know who it was."

Dana grabbed her phone out of her desk drawer and started tapping on it. Then she stopped and clutched the phone to her chest. "I can't watch."

"Of course not. You don't have to." I waved my hands. "But can you listen?"

Reluctantly, Dana pulled up an app that connected with her video system and scrolled back to yesterday, shortly before the party. I dragged a chair next to her so I could see.

"This is the only camera I have in the lobby area." She handed me the phone.

The camera was angled to see the front door and room, already decorated for the party. Half of the bottom part of the staircase was also visible, but the dining area was not in view. Even so, Polly's voice talking about the shish kebab on the menu was loud and clear, as were her footsteps retreating to the kitchen.

Moments later, people's legs came into the picture, coming down the stairs. Then Carla, the caterer, spoke. "I told him to pay me half up front, and now I'm worried I won't get paid at all. Then I'll be out the cost of the food plus my time."

"I tried to warn you. Even if the lawyer pays him, it doesn't mean he'll pay you." This person was still not on camera.

"You're the one who got me this gig."

"Don't worry. Mark my words. Mason will get what's coming to him. Some guy almost came to blows with him earlier. Trust me, no one likes him."

Then, the pair split up, and a side view of a man was visible as he walked through the front room toward the door.

Dana gasped, even though she still refused to look.

"There!" I tapped the screen to pause the video. "Did you hear that?"

"Who was it?"

"Can you just take a quick look?" I angled the phone towards her.

She swallowed, then turned her face toward the frozen video. A man with tousled brown hair was on screen, maybe in his late twenties or early thirties. Though the picture was good, it wasn't perfect, making it hard to pick out details.

Dana hesitated before shaking her head. "He might be familiar. I just don't know."

"Was he at the party?" I willed her to come up with more information.

"There were so many people. I...I..." She shrugged, then grabbed her phone back with shaky fingers.

"Can you send me a copy of this?"

She bit her lip. "Do you really need it?"

"I think it's a pretty strong lead."

"Okay, give me your email."

Moments later, my phone buzzed with the incoming video.

Dana dropped her phone on her desk. "Are you going to the police?"

"Of course." Well, I would after I downloaded it and made a secure copy for myself. Then I could compare it to the pictures I took last night and see if there was a match for the man. "By the way," I said as I tapped my phone. "What was the caterer doing upstairs with this guy?"

"I wish I knew." Dana released a weary sigh.

"I know this is bad timing, but do you mind if we get a cleaning company to come finish up in the kitchen?" I waved my phone at her. "I want to get right on this."

"There's no way I can afford that. But don't worry. I'll figure it out."

I mentally tallied what was in my savings account, then decided to bite the bullet. "I'll get you a cleaning crew." Even if their names were Polly, Naomi, and Lulu. "You can pay me back later."

Right now, there were more important things to focus on—like finding Mason's killer.

Chapter Eleven

FOR SOME STRANGE REASON, Verity decided it was more important to spend the rest of her evening hanging out with David instead of helping me figure out who the jean-clad man was. As for Polly, by the time I got home, she was already conked out for the night.

That left me to start investigating on my own—well, me and the pooches. It was just as well since I'd had a long day, and the only things that sounded good were PJs and hot cocoa with marshmallows.

After showering, I curled up on the couch near the window with the view of the B&B. Dana's house was dark—at least the part visible from here. It was almost nine o'clock, so she'd probably already gone to stay with her friend. (*If* someone who wasn't around to help with a massive cleanup after the murder of a loved one could really be called a friend.)

Pooh Bear trotted over to the couch and hopped up. I scratched behind his ears as he settled himself on my feet. Cujo scampered over, too, and yipped. "Come here, little fella." I scooped him off the floor and placed him on my lap. With both pooches on me, it made it hard to balance my tablet to get started, but I'd spent so much time away from them, it only seemed fair to give them some attention.

Eventually, they drifted off to sleep, and the house was quiet. Outside, an owl hooted from a nearby tree. Briefly, I wondered how James was getting along at my place. Hopefully, he wasn't making a mess and using up all my towels. But, for all the friction between us, he still had a good side to him.

Maybe that was why I wanted to clear James's name, besides wanting him to leave so I could move things along with Hamson. Even after Verity tried to create doubt as to James's innocence, I knew in my heart he wasn't capable of such an act. Besides, he didn't really have a motive. He may have been defending me from Mason's leering eyes and rude comments, but I had a sneaking suspicion much of that was for show.

Gently, I lifted Cujo off my lap and placed him next to Pooh Bear so he could stay warm. Then I opened my phone and transferred the video of Carla and the mystery man to my tablet. But before I played the clip, I needed to get my thoughts in order. I tapped open the notes app and did a brain dump.

First, Carla and her man friend were upset. Plus, they were upstairs in the B&B for no apparent reason. She was the first person I needed to talk to. I could go to her place of business tomorrow under the guise of letting her know she could pick up her catering equipment and old food, which would also help clear out the disaster in the dining area and kitchen. Two birds, one stone.

Second, someone in the crowd at the party had called out James. That person had been there during the argument between James and Mason. What else did that person know? Were they covering up for themselves? I had to figure out who that person was.

Third, the killer had to have crossed paths with James at the electrical breaker box. I needed to check back with him to see if he could remember any further details. Also, I should ask Dana if there was a camera in the kitchen, even though I didn't remember seeing one. Surely the police would have asked for that footage, given the importance of the electricity going out.

Which reminded me that the person I'd seen leaving in a huff the first time I'd gone to the B&B was an electrician. Or had he been a contractor? I scraped my memory, trying to recall what happened that day. Was it someone else who wasn't getting timely payments?

The person who'd told me about Mason having a problem with money had been Randall Wilson, the jeweler. He seemed to know a lot about Mason, *and* he'd been at the party. I tapped out a reminder to talk to him. I could go there under the guise of the jewelry store's winter extravaganza coming up, which I actually needed to sketch out ideas for.

I took a sip of my now-cold hot cocoa and set the mug down with a clatter. Pooh Bear opened one eye and snorted, as if to chide me for disturbing his rest.

Glancing over my notes, I realized I had a lot more trails to follow than I thought. If I could get the gang together, we could divvy up the tasks and work faster. Aunt Lulu still had some resistance to getting involved, but she was as curious as the rest of us and wanted the real killer caught.

The grandfather clock downstairs softly chimed nine times. I yawned and rubbed my gritty eyes. Last night's meeting with the gang and the early morning with Griff was starting to catch up with me. Yet, I still had investigating to do, even though it wasn't as much fun doing it alone. Or without snacks.

I opened the video on my tablet and watched it. Then watched again. And a third time. When that didn't produce an a-ha moment, I grabbed my earbuds and cranked up the volume. Still, nothing new.

Maybe the pictures I'd taken last night would prove more fruitful. I transferred them from my phone to my tablet and went through them slowly, enlarging each one to scan the faces for any resemblance to Carla's man friend. Finally, I found him in the conga line—at least I thought it was him. It was hard to tell with the party hat covering his hair. The mystery man on the video had a connection to Carla, Mason, and the law firm.

Quickly, I dialed up Verity. "Hey, I found something."

"Can it wait?" Music sounded in the background. "We're watching a movie."

"*Ver-i-ty*! I need you." The dogs stirred. I lowered my voice. "I think I found the guy who was with Carla in my pictures from the party."

"Have you turned it all over to the police?"

"Not yet. I was thinking of calling Hamson tomorrow."

"If you don't do it right away, they'll think you're withholding evidence." She giggled, then spoke in a muffled tone. "David, I'll be off the phone in just a minute. You can hold your horses." Another giggle.

"I'd rather hold you."

Gross.

"Okay, okay. I'll touch base tomorrow." I disconnected before I had to listen to any more of their shenanigans.

IT TURNED out that getting in touch with Hamson was easy. The next day, Verity called me from the library to tell me he was there and that if I hurried, I'd catch him.

But he wasn't all I caught—Officer Leon was with him. She gave me a warning glance when I asked to speak to him alone. To be fair, since it was official business, I probably should have included her.

"Come find me outside in ten," he said to me, sensing his partner's reluctance. He motioned to Officer Leon with his head, and together they walked out the front door. Library patrons seemed to breathe a sigh of relief when they left. As for me, I sighed with longing.

I edged over to Verity, who manned the reference desk. "What was that all about?"

"A fight broke out between two patrons, and someone called it in. I mean, if someone had just come to me, I'd have taken care of it." She wheeled her hands around like she was going to chop someone's head off.

I thought of all the punishing takedowns she'd taught me (that I mostly didn't remember) and agreed with her. Then I pulled out my phone and opened the gallery to show her the picture I'd discovered last night. "This guy right here. Have you seen him?"

Verity leaned down and peered closely. "He looks vaguely familiar. I see a lot of people here, but I can't really place him."

"That's the same thing Dana said. Maybe I'll have better luck with Hamson." I tucked my phone away and yawned. It was definitely time for more coffee and maybe a pastry. "Can you meet for lunch later?"

She shook her head, then spoke while simultaneously typing on the keyboard. "David and I are meeting. How about getting together with everyone for dinner?"

We agreed on a time to meet at Polly's house, even though I hadn't confirmed it with my host. I didn't think she'd mind as long as I provided the food. Hopefully, I could persuade all the ladies to meet. If I hustled this afternoon, I might even have more to report.

Though it hadn't been ten minutes, I went outside to track Hamson down. The sight of him smiling broadly in the sunlight made my breath hitch. He and his partner exchanged another quip, and both grinned and nodded in that reserved way that was friendly, yet cop-like.

As I approached, Officer Leon nodded at me curtly. "I'll just be across the street getting some ice cream." She headed toward Walter's shop, Yum Yum's.

Without removing his sunglasses, Hamson turned to me and spoke, his professional veneer firmly in place. "All right, Crumb. What's on your mind?"

"Crumb?" I raised my eyebrows at him and blinked. "That's what you're calling me now?"

He tucked his thumbs into his belt loops and eased back on his heels. "What would you like me to call you?"

Mrs. Hamson.

No—wait. Where did that come from? I needed more sleep. Or something. Heat traveled up my neck and settled in my cheeks. I slid my sunglasses on to hide myself. "Never mind. There's something I forgot to tell you the other night."

"Here, let's get in the shade. Your face is red." He ushered me over to a park bench under a tree. Then he motioned for me to sit first. "Now, tell me what you forgot. Is it about the case?"

"Of course it's about the case. What else would I be talking about?"

Hamson adjusted his bullet-resistant vest, then settled his elbows on his knees. "The other night, you took our conversation a little…off track."

"Me? I wasn't the one asking about my so-called boyfriend. If I didn't know better, I'd think you were a teensy bit jealous." I pinched my fingers together for emphasis.

"I used the term to clarify who—"

"You could've used his name or even called him man bun like everyone else."

Hamson cleared his throat. "Let's get back to what you came to tell me. The last time I saw you, you remembered something about an electrician."

"Yeah, did you follow up on that?"

He held up his hand. "We're checking out several leads."

"I get that's the *official* line, but c'mon. I'm the one who gave you the tip. The least you could do is give me a follow-up."

"If you'll recall, I also told you I'm not really in the investigation. The state police took over." A look of regret flashed over his face, at least from what I could tell with his sunglasses still on. "How about you tell me what else you remembered, then I can pass it along to those guys."

"Fine." I slid closer to him until our arms brushed.

A hint of a smile ghosted his lips. "What are you doing?"

"Showing you a video." It was my turn to sound professional and uninterested, which took a lot of work on my part, especially with his cologne rolling off him in citrusy waves with hints of the sea. I inhaled deeply and—

"KC?"

"Oh, right." I glanced around to ensure our privacy, then pulled out my phone and loaded the video. "You're not going to believe this."

Once it began to play, Hamson leaned in to hear the conversation on my phone over the chatter of the kids playing frisbee behind us on the courthouse lawn. When it finished, he sat straight and pulled off his sunglasses. "Who is that?"

"I was hoping you'd know." I swiped away from the video and pulled up the clearest picture I had of the mystery man. "This is the same guy."

Hamson leaned closer and shaded the screen with his hand. "It's a little hard to tell."

"Do you recognize him at all? In a town the size of Beaver Bluff, I'm sure you've had contact with a lot of people."

"He looks familiar, but I can't really place him."

That's what everyone seemed to think. "Would you like me to send you these pictures? Then we'd have a better shot at figuring out who this guy is." I started swiping. "Even if he has nothing to do with the murder, he obviously knows many people who had a bone to pick with Mason."

"KC." Hamson gently lifted the sunglasses from my face and set them on my head. "There is no we."

I prayed he only meant as far as the case was concerned. I set the phone on my lap. "Sorry, I forgot. But you want me to send these to you, right?"

"Of course. Send them to the same address as the pictures from the other night." Hamson stood, shading me with his rugged figure. "I'm not sure how relevant this information is, but it's always helpful to have more leads."

At least he was taking my information seriously. That was progress.

I stood, too. "All right. I guess we'll…see you around."

Hamson patted my shoulder, then walked toward the ice cream shop. My heart sank a fraction as I watched him leave. But the sinking feeling was quickly replaced by a sense of purpose.

It was time to question the jeweler.

Chapter Twelve

WILSON'S JEWELERS was surprisingly busy for a Sunday after-noon. A young couple leaned over one display, hugging on each other. The young man who'd bought an engagement ring the other day stood near Randall at a different glass case. And an elderly gentleman checked out the jewelry near the front window alongside a lady who appeared to work there.

So much for trying to get time with the owner to ferret out information.

Randall looked over at me and held up a finger. "I'll be with you shortly."

"No rush." I smiled.

How would I get him alone long enough to find out what he knew about Mason's debts? I took out my tablet and opened the notes app to refresh my memory about the winter extravaganza. If I couldn't talk about the murder, I could at least get some real work done.

"If I could just get my money back," the guy at the counter pleaded as he pulled a velvet box out of his jeans pocket.

Ouch. She must've said no.

Randall spoke in a much softer tone. "As I said, there's really nothing I can do."

"Her controlling family butted in, and now she can't get married." The guy raked his hands through his shaggy hair. "Come on, Randall, I thought we were friends."

"We are, but this is business. I'm terribly sorry." Remorse laced Randall's voice.

I turned back to my tablet and tried to tune them out. I'd already set up two basic social media accounts for the jewelry store, which had a total of five followers, two of which were Verity and me. I needed Randall to start pushing his social media with his new customers. Maybe we could implement a drawing for a free…I glanced around…what could he give away? I made a note to discuss it with him.

My phone buzzed in my pocket. A text from James.

James: *do you have any food here?*

Me: *No*

James: *Booze?*

Me: *No! You can go to the store and buy stuff. You're not on house arrest!!!*

James: *Cool. Do you want to go with me?*

Me: *NO!!! I'm working.*

I closed the messaging app, determined not to look at the phone when it buzzed again in my hand. His text reminded me of another reason James could never have murdered Mason. If he couldn't even figure out lunch, he could never figure out how to cover up a murder. However, I didn't think that defense would hold up in court.

"KC, how are you?" Randall stood on the opposite side of the display case where I'd set myself up to work.

The shop had only two customers left—the lovey-dovey couple. I'd been so irritated with James that I hadn't heard everyone else leave. I closed the cover of my tablet. "It's been a strange couple of days."

"Indeed, it has. Would you like to come to my office?" Randall indicated the small swinging gate I could pass through to get to the back.

I followed him through a door behind the counter, then into a narrow workspace with a table and several gadgets. "Do you make jewelry back here?"

"No," Randall said over his shoulder as he entered a room in the very back. "But I do offer jewelry repair and resizing, that type of thing. Come and make yourself comfortable." He gestured to a chair wedged next to a desk inside his windowless office.

"That was sure some party Friday night." I sat and opened my tablet on his desk.

He dropped onto his rolling chair and blew a raspberry. "You're telling me. I thought we'd never get out of there. Brenda's been pretty upset ever since it happened."

Randall didn't have to explain what "it" was. The unsettling images ran through my head once again, as they often did, no matter how hard I tried to shut them out.

I shifted in my seat and attempted to study his face without him taking notice. "Did your wife know Mason well?"

Worry lines creased Randall's forehead. "She may have known him in passing. It was just…she doesn't like the sight of blood." He nervously worked the buttons on his flannel vest. "I mean, this was the stuff of nightmares. Know what I mean?"

"Totally." I looked away, hoping he'd feel more free to answer if I didn't pin him with my gaze. "Tell me, how did you know Mason? Before I left here last time, you warned me to get paid up front. I'll be honest—I should've taken your advice."

Randall issues a mirthless laugh. "He stiffed you, too, eh?"

"Is that what he did, stiff you?" I bit my lip, hoping the jeweler didn't think I was implying he was to blame for Mason's murder.

"No way, no how." Randall's chair squeaked as he leaned back and palmed his chest. "I get my payments up front, cash or credit."

"Oh, considering the advice you gave me, I figured you'd had a bad experience with Mason." I drew in a breath of stale air and wondered how to get more intel from the jeweler. This questioning stuff was harder than it looked.

"I may not be the hub of Beaver Bluff like your bakery, but I hear things. Good things, bad things, all kinds of things. People talk." His mouth tilted in a half-smile. "And if there's one thing I'm good at, it's listening."

"Did you tell the police who you'd heard talk about Mason? You might have information that would lead to the killer."

He picked up a pen off his desk and started clicking the end of it. "Well, I don't know about that. Being owed money is one thing, but would anyone kill for that?"

"I guess that depends on how much he owed."

Randall's mouth turned down as he considered my words. "Good point. Now, what have you got to show me?"

For the next twenty minutes, we went over the social media accounts and my ideas for gaining more followers. Then we talked about expanding the promotional opportunities for his winter extravaganza and what he could offer to lure in more customers. We even discussed potential partnerships with other local businesses to increase his visibility.

When we were ready to wrap up, Randall grinned. "I'm telling you, you are worth your weight in gold, KC. And believe me, I know the value of gold."

I laughed at his silly jeweler joke. "In that case, I'd appreciate any referrals you could send my way."

"Yeah, sure thing." He stood, effectively dismissing me.

"Just one more thing." I opened the gallery on my tablet and pulled up the picture of Carla's mystery man. "Do you know who this person is?"

Randall craned his neck over my shoulder. "Wait, was this taken at the party?"

I swiped the screen. "Yeah, and this one here was taken—"

"Whoa." He stood back and held up his hands. A dark expression clouded his eyes. "I already told the cops everything I know. I'm not sure why you're asking questions, too."

I quickly switched off the tablet. "So, you *do* know him?"

"I didn't say that." Randall ran his hand through his thick black hair.

"He just looks familiar, perhaps?"

The jeweler's mouth tightened. "Look, you want my advice? Stay out of it. Nothing good ever comes of poking around in other people's business."

Never mind that he'd been the one talking about others in the first place.

"Have a good day." Randall's words didn't match his tone as he opened the door and motioned for me to leave.

I hoped I hadn't lost a client, but I was pretty sure I'd lost a lead.

AFTER LEAVING WILSON'S JEWELERS, I headed back to the library to regroup. Verity worked a short line of patrons asking how to download e-books and needing help with the public computers. I joined the queue since there was no other way I could talk to her. Finally, I got to the front.

"What's up?" Verity kept her eyes trained on the computer monitor while she typed and talked.

"I had a very interesting chat at the jewelry store." I set my handbag on the counter.

She stopped typing. "You'll have to tell me about it later. It's kind of busy."

"I happen to have a reference question."

Verity tilted her head and gave me a knowing look. "A real reference question?"

"Can you find the contact information for Carla's Catering? That's my next stop." I hated that I had to sleuth alone. Maybe I could rope Polly into joining me, and we'd bring my pooches along for the ride.

"I'm pretty sure you could've looked that up yourself."

"Is that how you treat all your patrons?" I smirked.

"Fine. I will pull up their website." Verity typed, then frowned, then typed some more. "Let me just get rid of this pop-up. Okay, the website only has a phone number and a way to contact them by email."

"I'd prefer to go see her in person. Got an address?"

"Not on their website. Let me check this reference database." Her fingers flew expertly across the keys while I waited. A short line formed behind me, but Verity continued helping me. "Interesting. They aren't listing a physical address here, either."

"There has to be a way." I drummed my fingers on the counter. "Use your voodoo, or whatever it is you do."

"I could see who the domain is registered to, and they might list an address. Hang on a sec." She continued searching, then moments later shook her head. "They're listing an address out of California. I'm sorry, but you might be out of luck."

"Wait, I know." I snapped my fingers. "I just remembered something."

The person in line behind me groaned.

"It'll just take a minute," I said to them before refocusing my attention on Verity. "You said there was a pop-up on the website. Can you go back and see if it's for a newsletter?"

Verity pulled the Carla's Catering website back up. "Yes, it says that if you join the newsletter, you'll get exclusive deals, yada-yada."

"Great. Let's join the newsletter because once they send an email, it'll have a physical address at the bottom. It's a requirement for email marketing." I pointed at her screen and motioned for her to hurry. "Just put your email address in."

"I don't want to join the list." Verity grimaced.

"One of us has to."

The person behind me groaned again, this time a little louder.

"I'll put in yours. That way, you'll have the address as soon as possible." Verity smiled as she tapped the keys. "There we go. Let me know what you find out. And remember…" She wheeled her hands around in a self-defense-type motion. "Always be alert, especially since you'll be by yourself."

I didn't think Carla would be a danger to me. Then again, she was the one who brought the stainless-steel skewers in the first place.

I stepped out of line and pulled out my phone. Hopefully, since Carla knew enough about marketing to set up an email newsletter, she also had an auto-responding sequence set up. That way, I would get an email sooner rather than later.

Outside, the afternoon sun shone brightly, and it was hard to believe that winter was fast approaching. I walked across the street to the courtyard and scanned the area. Sadly, Hamson and Officer Leon were nowhere to be found, not that he would have taken the time to talk to me twice. At least not with his partner looking over his shoulder.

I dodged a kid on a scooter and headed for the park bench to rest for a minute. No sooner had I sat than my phone pinged with an incoming email. Sure enough, Carla's newsletter arrived. I quickly opened it and scrolled past the offer for a free dessert with my first catering order over seventy-five dollars.

As predicted, her physical address was at the bottom. I copied and pasted it into the maps app. Vine Street, two blocks over from the town square, well within walking distance. I studied the directions, then started to cross the road. A horn blasted me from the side.

I screamed and caught my breath as a dark, shiny Lincoln Town Car halted. I clutched my chest as my heart threatened to explode. The driver and I stared at each other, then both of us shook our fists.

The driver was Polly.

Chapter Thirteen

"GET in before someone runs you over," Polly shouted out her window.

"You mean like *you*?" I hurried to the passenger side as another car stopped behind her and another one behind them. The third one back tooted their horn. I smiled and waved at them while opening the door.

Pooh Bear woofed at me. He preferred to ride shotgun, so I shut that door and then climbed into the backseat next to Cujo instead.

"Hello, my little fluff ball." I ruffled his ears and cuddled him to my chest.

Polly stepped on the gas. "What were you doing in the middle of the road? I was coming downtown to look for you, but I didn't expect to see you there."

"I was chasing a lead." I fastened my seatbelt. "Maybe you should slow down a bit. The dogs aren't strapped in."

"Pooh Bear likes the way I drive, don't you, boy?"

He released a bark of agreement.

"Who are we chasing, anyway? They don't stand a chance against my car." Polly patted the dashboard.

"We're not chasing a person, just a lead."

"Aww, shucks. That would've been fun." She shook her head in dismay, then she caught my gaze in the rearview mirror. "Where to?"

I pulled up the address and gave it to Polly. "What have you and the boys been up to today?"

"A little of this, a little of that. I called Naomi to see if she wanted to meet me for lunch, but she was with Walter. Then I called your Aunt Lulu to see if she wanted to get together, but she texted she was still in church," Polly sighed. "So, then I thought we'd come and find you."

"Glad to know I was the last choice."

"Oh, please. Spare me the pity party. We live together for the moment, so it's not like we don't have plenty of time with each other." She wheeled around a corner, one street over from Vine. "What's at this address we're going to, anyway? Are we tracking someone? Will we need to rough them up?"

"Good grief, no." At least, I hoped not. I stroked Cujo's fur as I formulated a plan. "But let's slow down and try to blend in, so we don't scare them away."

Polly reluctantly took her foot off the gas as we entered a neighborhood with big trees and old houses. "Who are we trying not to scare away?"

"Carla, from Carla's Catering. But it doesn't look like there are any businesses here." I glanced at my phone to verify the address. "We're looking for twenty-seven thirteen."

We checked out the addresses on the houses as we passed each one. Polly pointed. "It's got to be that one across the street. You know, sometimes people run businesses out of their houses until they can afford to rent a spot."

"Pull over. I kind of want to scope the place out before I talk to her."

Polly eased next to the curb, rolled the windows down halfway, and shut off the engine. "Too bad I don't have my binoculars."

I agreed. It was hard to see much without being totally obvious. The outside of the house carried a 1970s vibe, complete with a painted brick front and a one-car garage. Unless Carla lived alone, I imagined it would be hard to run a business from the tiny home.

"Can you give me some details? I don't even know why we're here." Polly glanced over her shoulder at me.

"I'd like to let her know she can pick up her catering stuff from the B&B."

"Okay, that's the cover. And what's the real reason?"

"To find out who that guy was with her the day of the party. Not only did he make comments about Mason before the big shindig, but he was also there when Mason was murdered."

"You found him in the pictures?" Excitement lit Polly's voice, causing Pooh Bear's ears to perk up. "Was he anywhere near the kitchen when the lights went out?"

"That's the problem—I don't have any pictures from just before the lights went out. My photos show who was there, but not their exact position when Mason was killed."

A breeze blew through the car, and we enjoyed a quiet moment despite our grisly topic. Unfortunately, Mason's murder had taken up all my mental bandwidth lately, and I had a feeling that wouldn't change until we caught the killer.

"Whoever it was had to have been close to the kitchen when the lights went out. It was so dark, they wouldn't have been able to walk over, find Mason, and nail him with that level of accuracy if they'd just been in the crowd." Polly grinned, pleased with herself.

"You make a good point. But anyone could've grabbed a skewer, slipped into the kitchen, cut the lights, and stabbed Mason." I racked my brain, trying to recreate the scene in my mind.

Who all had been standing in the front room right as the lights went off? Those would be the guests who were innocent. The problem was, I hadn't paid close attention to all the people I didn't know. I remember seeing Griff and Holly, Benson Michaels, and a bunch of random party-goers.

"And they could've also slipped back out of the kitchen and

blended into the crowd before you turned on your flashlight." Polly rubbed Pooh Bear's ears.

"Could they, though? They would've been covered in blood, too, wouldn't they?" I grimaced at the thought.

"Maybe not covered, per se." Polly drew in a sharp breath, then whipped around in her seat so she could look me in the eye. "Unless they were wearing an *apron*." Her eyes swept back and forth between me and Carla's house. "Anyone wearing an apron could have chucked it off somewhere."

"Yikes. Do you remember seeing Carla after the murder? And did she still have on her apron?" I'd have to go back through my pictures and look for her, although, as we'd already discussed, seeing someone in the photo didn't necessarily mean they didn't slip away and kill Mason.

"She was back and forth between the dining room and the kitchen, but I don't remember specifically seeing her afterward." Polly's eyes rounded.

"But even if she took off the apron, the police would have found it," I reasoned.

Polly's eyes narrowed. "Who says they didn't?"

Who, indeed? It wasn't as if Hamson was keeping me in the loop. But according to him, he wasn't necessarily in the loop, either. Was Carla the only one wearing an apron that day? She was the only one from her company there, and from the looks of her house/business, she was likely a one-woman show.

I shook off the thought. "I think we've gotten off-track. I agree that whoever killed Mason would likely have blood on them, but that doesn't mean we're looking for discarded aprons. We can't just make up clues."

Polly shrugged, seemingly fine with letting go of that theory. "Okay. Why don't you go ahead and talk to her, and I'll wait here with the pooches."

I scooted over until I was directly behind the driver's seat so I could see Carla's place better. There was no movement, nor was there a car in the driveway. Maybe she wasn't even home. "It couldn't hurt. I have a perfectly legitimate reason for talking to her. She really does need to pick up her catering stuff."

Which reminded me, I still needed to call a professional service to help Dana clean up the B&B. I tapped a reminder into my phone. Maybe I could find a crime-scene cleaner from the city. It would be expensive, but it didn't sound like something Dana could do for herself. Too bad her so-called friend wasn't stepping up to help.

"Here goes nothing." I scooped Cujo off my lap and handed him to Polly. Then I climbed out of the car, steeled my confidence, and walked across the street. This time I looked both ways.

My heels clacked against the sidewalk as I approached the decrepit house. The wind whistled through the surrounding trees, but the neighborhood itself was devoid of noise. No children playing or dogs barking. A chill slithered down my spine as I reached the front door.

The plastic doorbell had yellowed over time, and when I pressed it, nothing happened. Instead, I lifted my hand and knocked on the splintery door. My knock was met with silence. I glanced behind me at Polly and Pooh Bear peering through the car window and shrugged.

Once again, I knocked.

Maybe Carla was out at a catering job. If she didn't answer, I'd have to resort to calling, to at least ask her to pick up her supplies. That would be one less thing for Dana to handle. But I'd really wanted to see her in person.

I craned my neck to look through the open window near the front door. Sunlight glinted off the glass, obscuring my view. If only I could see, then maybe I'd be able to confirm this was Carla's place.

Once more, I glanced over my shoulder at the quiet neighborhood. The sidewalks were empty, as well as the street.

Slowly, I edged off the porch, my heel partially sinking into the neglected flowerbed. I reached for the protruding windowsill to balance myself as I took another step. Finally, I had a clear view.

Inside, soda cans and potato chip bags littered the coffee table, and a pile of rumpled blankets covered the couch. Precariously balanced takeout boxes sat on an end table next to the remote control. If this was Carla's place, she didn't seem to be a fan of her own cuisine.

If I could see down the hall, maybe I'd be able to—

"Hey, what are you doing?" A male voice reverberated off the brick walls.

I jumped back, my heart lodged in my throat. It took me a moment to gain my bearings as I looked for the person who'd spoken.

"Why are you looking in the window?" The figure emerged from the side of the house. As he drew closer, familiarity sparked inside me. Where did I know him from? He walked closer with the swagger of someone about to strike.

Then it hit me—I was face-to-face with Carla's jean-clad man. He was shorter than I expected, but his higher-pitched voice was a perfect match. It was definitely him.

My thoughts raced as I grasped for a reasonable excuse. Slowly, I stepped away from the window. "Hey, there. I was checking to see if Carla was around."

"By looking in the window?" The young man's voice shifted from angry to wary.

"Oh, yeah…you know Carla." I shrugged, realizing my comment made no sense whatsoever but hoping he'd roll with it.

He tilted his head, giving me time to study his features. Tousled brownish hair with a shapeless cut and a wispy beard that hadn't been clear on the video but was now obvious in the after-noon sunlight.

The man's shoulders relaxed. "She ain't here."

"I kind of guessed that." I motioned to the window. "Do you know when she'll be back?"

"Whatcha need?"

"Oh…catering stuff." I relaxed and tried to match his casual posture. If I could catch him off guard, maybe I could learn something. "Are you her assistant?"

"Sometimes."

"Her…friend?"

His eyes narrowed. "Sometimes."

My fishing expedition was getting me nowhere. I decided to change tactics. "Hey, you look familiar. Have we met?"

"Uh-uh. I don't remember you."

It was a little sad to know my black dress had not drawn the attention I thought it would the other night. However, the fact that he didn't remember me might work to my advantage by him not realizing I'd been at the party, too, and was now trying to get intel. I smiled. "I'm KC. And you are…"

"Kai." I glanced back to the side of the house. "I gotta get back to my thing."

My chance to quiz this guy was slipping away. I willed myself to find a way to connect. "Maybe I'll give Carla a call. I kind of need her advice."

"Cool." He stuffed his hands inside his pockets, causing his jeans to ride lower on his waist. "See ya."

"I had this job that I'm not getting paid for, and I think she has the same problem."

Kai snorted. "That seems to be going around."

"The guy up and died on me."

He stiffened, his shoulders drawing higher.

"But as I hear it, he wasn't likely to pay up, anyway." I tilted my head and raised my eyebrows. "If you know what I mean."

Kai eased backward. "I don't know what you're talking about."

"That Mason guy that…" I slit my finger across my throat to make the point.

Panic flickered in Kai's eyes. He continued walking backward, still facing me. "Lady, I don't know what you want, but you… you…" His Adam's apple bobbed with a hard swallow.

Then he turned and ran.

Chapter Fourteen

I SPRINTED across the front yard after Kai, my heels kicking up dirt behind me. At least I'd worn the two-inchers, which gave me a fighting chance. When I reached the sidewalk, I increased my speed and tried to ignore the back of my dress, flipping around with every step.

Kai dashed down the sidewalk. For a shorter guy, he moved fast. His headstart afforded him a ten-yard gap, but I was gaining quickly despite my throbbing feet.

He passed the neighbor's house and leaped over a tricycle on the sidewalk. Moments later, I slowed down to skirt around the toy, allowing Kai to widen the distance between us. Then we ran past the second house, where an elderly couple watched us from chairs on their porch.

"Kai, stop! I just want to talk!" My shouts seemed to inspire him to move faster.

I pumped my arms harder and willed myself to catch up. My heart jack-hammered inside my chest, and my lungs burned. But I couldn't let Kai go. He was my first real lead and could very well be the killer.

A dark car slowly rolled up beside me, and a dog barked. It sounded like Pooh Bear, but I didn't dare take the time to look.

"Why don't you hop into the car?" Polly asked as she crept along to match my pace. Perhaps I wasn't moving as fast as I thought.

Then Kai peeled around a driveway and darted between two houses on a narrow path.

"Because you can't go…" I pointed, too out of breath to talk. I left the sidewalk and followed Kai down the small alley.

He pulled farther ahead, no doubt because he was in sneakers. I tried to keep pace, hoping I didn't lose my footing on the gravel. Ahead, a brick wall blocked his way. Kai glanced over his shoulder, his unkempt hair momentarily covering his eyes.

"There's nowhere…for you to go!" I huffed, my lungs crushed.

Fierce barks pierced the air behind me. Then beside me. The sound of paws on gravel accompanied the barks. Suddenly, Pooh Bear blew past me, focused on his target.

Kai sprinted, then launched himself on top of a trash bin. He grasped the top of the wall and hoisted himself over just as Pooh Bear caught up. Pooh jumped and barked until I got there to calm him.

I ruffled his fur. "It's okay, boy." I glanced at the trash bin Kai had used to help scale the wall and weighed my options. The odds of me making it over the top and landing on the other side in one piece were pretty small.

My phone rang inside my pocket. Verity. "Hey."

"I'm on a break now. Just wanted to see if you'd turned anything else up."

I bent over, bracing my free hand on my knee. "I've been chasing a lead down Vine Street."

"Like actual chasing?"

"Yeah." *Huff, puff.*

"Well, don't let me stop you. Keep going!"

"I can't." I panted and wiped the sweat from my eyes. "I'm out of gas."

THE EXCITEMENT of finally having the gang all together that night overshadowed the disappointment of losing Kai. With everyone going their separate ways lately, I'd missed my friends. For the first time ever, we gathered at Polly's place since James still occupied mine. That was fine. Polly had better snacks.

We gathered in her upstairs parlor with a view of the B&B. It was hard not to keep looking out the window at the dark Victorian. Was Dana still staying with her friend? Without having her house fully cleaned yet, I sure hoped so.

"Walter and I were hoping to have an engagement party so we could celebrate with everyone, but with all this murder business, I don't think that's going to happen." Naomi sighed, then offered a piece of her blueberry muffin to Pooh Bear. He nuzzled her as a way of saying thanks.

"We could have a party at one of our places. It doesn't have to be fancy." Polly smiled with quivering lips, and I could tell she was doing her best to be supportive, even though she missed her best friend.

I handed Cujo to Polly for support. "We'll figure something out, and it'll be fantastic."

Aunt Lulu yawned. "Let's get down to business. I've got an early morning. I've added peppermint cinnamon rolls to the menu as we head towards the holidays, so that'll take extra time."

We all oohed and made plans to be there bright and early. I took a moment to grab a muffin and fill my coffee cup. Between the investigation, starting a business, and working at Crumb's, my caffeine addiction was completely justified.

"I'm still not sure how I feel about all of us mucking around in this investigation." Lulu's forehead wrinkled. "Honestly, KC, your mother would throttle me if she knew I wasn't doing something to stop you."

Somehow, I doubted that.

"You say that every time, but everything seems to work out." Naomi reached across the couch and patted Lulu's hand.

"Besides, we do a faster job of it than the police," Polly said matter-of-factly. She turned to me. "Nothing against Hamson, of course."

"According to him, he's not really involved. The state police were called back in. But to your point, I think we've been able to solve the murders more quickly than the police because we work well together, and we don't have to play by all the same rules they do." I fiddled with the legs of the easel, trying to angle it so everyone could see.

"On the flip side, we don't have access to all the information." Lulu worried the handle of her teacup. "Or the resources, like protection. I can't help but think about what happened to KC last time when she got hit on the head."

No way did I want a repeat of that. At the same time, we had to move this investigation along. I needed my house back.

"This time, we all need to stick together. No one—and I mean *no one*—goes off on their own." Naomi's puffy white hair trembled when she spoke.

Everyone swung their gazes to me.

I held up my hands. "Fine, fine. It's just that some of us—" I looked pointedly at Naomi and Verity. "Seem to have our minds on *other things*." Namely, men. "If we're going to work as a team, we all need to be available."

The gang volleyed blame back and forth until Polly whistled through her fingers. "How about we focus on the crime board and splitting up the tasks? I believe Verity has something for us."

Verity reached behind her chair and pulled out a medium-sized dry erase board. "Voila. Here's what I came up with this afternoon. It was kind of short notice, but this will get us started."

After my failed attempt to catch Kai, I'd sent Verity some photos and asked her to set up the crime board. With only Kai's and Carla's heads next to the picture of Mason, it seemed a little empty.

"Those are our only suspects?" Lulu motioned to the board with her teacup.

Naomi tsked and slowly shook her head. "Ohhh, we're not doing too well, are we."

"There's one more person who strikes me as a possible suspect, but I don't have his picture." I sat on the loveseat next to Polly. "The first time I went to the B&B, an electrician was there, and he was furious with Mason. Unfortunately, I have no idea who he was."

Verity drew a cartoonish man with a lightning bolt next to his head and wrote "electrician" underneath him. "Maybe you should ask Dana who that was."

I agreed. "I'll be happy to do that, but I think the bigger focus should be on Kai."

"Kai is the person on the board?" Lulu asked.

"Yes, so this is a picture from the night of the party." I pointed to his head and then pulled out my tablet and opened the gallery. "And here's one from just before that when he was talking with Carla. I got this one from the B&B's video. Even though this is a side view, you can see it's the same guy." I passed the tablet to Naomi, who then passed it to Lulu.

"You can't tell from the picture, but the perp is about five-foot-seven and one-hundred and seventy pounds. If only I'd let Pooh Bear out of the car a few seconds sooner, we'd have caught him." Polly fisted her hand.

"Does this gentleman work for the law firm?" Lulu poised her finger to her mouth as she studied the board.

"Gentleman?" Polly snorted. "He looks more like a perp."

We all groaned in unison.

"Let's not profile based on appearance." Verity tutted. "We need to work with cold, hard facts if we want to find the truth." The marker squeaked when she drew a line from Kai's head to the corner where she wrote "law firm" inside a circle.

"As of now, we don't know of any connection to the law firm. I believe he was at the party with Carla. He wasn't clear about his relation to her." I thought back to his vague answers this afternoon.

Verity drew an arrow between Kai and Carla.

"Was he mingling with the people at the party?" Naomi asked.

Polly nodded. "Probably so, since his picture came from a crowd shot. However, neither one of us noticed him in particular on that night."

"What do we know about Carla?" Lulu sipped her tea.

I stood next to the board to address everyone. "All we know about Carla is that she was worried about getting paid, and Kai said that a lot of people were upset with Mason and that he would get what was coming to him. Not only that," I said as I started to pace. "He mentioned seeing the argument between James and Mason. My question is, what was he doing at the B&B when he saw them? Also, he and Carla had been upstairs, which doesn't make any sense."

"It must've been him that shouted the accusation against 'man bun' from the crowd." Polly used her fingers for air quotes. "Which he *would* do to throw suspicion off himself."

"Good point," I said. "But would whoever shouted that have been able to get back into the room—in the dark, no less—after killing Mason?"

We all took a moment to ponder. I couldn't remember whether the swinging door to the kitchen sounded again after the time Mason's body fell through.

"So, are we suspecting Kai as the probable killer?" Lulu looked between each of us. "Do we know if he even had a motive?"

The dogs' heads moved back and forth as I continued pacing. "We don't, unless he's another person who Mason owed money to." I stopped. "Speaking of which, you know who else should be on the board? Randall Wilson, the jeweler."

"Why would he be a suspect? He was perfectly nice when he sold us my ring." Naomi grinned as she flashed her finger.

"I thought so too until he told me I shouldn't get involved

when I tried to fish for information." I shuddered, remembering the tone of his voice when he told me to stay out of it.

Verity uncapped the marker and drew a caricature of a man with a fat ring on his finger. She wrote "Randall" underneath it. "Do you think he might be directly involved? Was he even at the party?"

"Yes, he was. But I don't remember where he was standing when the lights went out." I stopped pacing and scratched my head. "When I talked to him previously, he seemed to know a lot about Mason owing people money."

Naomi nodded. "That's one of the biggest reasons people kill. At least in the detective novels I've been reading. Did Mason owe Randall money, too?"

"No, but that doesn't mean he didn't kill him for something else," I reasoned.

Lulu set her cup down and yawned. "Okay, so we know Kai is behaving suspiciously, but where do we go from here? It doesn't seem like there's a lot we can do."

The marker squealed again as Verity started writing bullet points. "First thing, KC needs to talk to Dana and ask about the electrician."

"I think we need to get eyes on Kai and Carla. Who's up for a stakeout?" Polly looked between us all.

"I have to be at the bakery early."

"Walter and I have plans."

"David is taking me out to dinner."

I threw my arms up. "You guys, we just talked about this. Remember? We have to work together. No one goes anywhere alone, yada-yada?"

"But this is last minute."

"I can't just cancel."

"Walter likes to cuddle at the end of the day—"

"Fine, fine, fine." I cut Naomi off before I had to hear any more details. "I'll go with Polly. But starting tomorrow, I expect full participation."

Judging by the blank expressions around the room, I wasn't sure I would get it.

Chapter Fifteen

IT WAS NEARLY eleven o'clock by the time Polly and I arrived at Carla's place. The wind rustled through the trees, and the moonless night made it difficult to see once we parked across the street and turned off the headlights.

"Which snacks do you want to start with?" Polly reached into the loaded beach bag at her feet on the passenger's side of my car. Even though we'd munched on pastries with the gang back at the house, we brought popcorn, pretzels, leftover pepperoni pizza, and diet soda. We were prepared for a long night.

"Popcorn, before it gets cold." I squinted into the darkness. The scant light from the neighbor's porch illuminated the words "Carla's Catering" on the side of the small SUV parked in the driveway.

Plastic crinkled as Polly dug around and pulled out the popcorn. "It's a good thing we left Pooh and Cujo home, or they'd be all over this."

The smell of butter wafted from the bag as I popped the first few kernels into my mouth. "We should probably feed them more actual dog food. I think they're getting spoiled."

"Nonsense. Who could say no to those little guys?" Polly

pointed to Carla's house. "Look, there's a shadow moving in the living room."

Unfortunately, the closed curtains left us with little to go on. I finished the buttery kernels before I spoke. "Wait, are there two of them?"

"Yeah, it has to be Carla and Kai." Polly shoveled a handful into her mouth.

"Not necessarily. I mean, we don't even know if Kai lives there, and it's pretty late for visitors."

"Do you think they're an item?"

"Hard to say, especially since Kai wasn't very specific when I talked to him earlier. And I don't remember them hanging out together at the party." I took a swig of soda. "Then again, I hadn't really noticed him. He was just another face in the crowd."

"I think we would've noticed if Carla had a boyfriend-type hanging all over her like Walter and Naomi do," Polly grunted.

I snorted back. "Not everyone is quite as affectionate as Naomi and Walter." Or Verity and David, for that matter. Lovebirds surrounded Polly and me. I grabbed a handful of popcorn and chewed faster to block the images. "Plus, Carla was working, so I doubt we'd have seen anything obvious. Even if they are a couple, it probably doesn't matter to the case, right?"

"Hmmm. Maybe, maybe not. Unless they were in cahoots, in which case they'll be covering for each other." Polly pulled out her binoculars. "Man, even with these, I can't get a bead on what they're doing in there."

I rolled my eyes. "They're binoculars, not x-ray vision goggles."

"Oh, I wonder if I should get a pair of those."

"I don't think that's a thing, Polly." I took another caffeinated gulp to ward off the sleepiness in my eyes. This whole investigation was exhausting. When it was all over, maybe I'd take a few days off from Crumb's and from my own business and chill out. Stream a few videos and take naps and—

"Is that a third person in there?" She adjusted the binoculars.

I sat up, bumping my bag against the steering wheel. Kernels fell to the floor. "It sure looks like it. Maybe it's a roommate situation."

"But there's only one car in the driveway."

"One more could be in the garage," I suggested.

Minutes passed as three shadowy figures moved back and forth across the living room. We watched in silence, frustration mounting over the fact that we had no idea what was going on behind the curtain.

"I'm still thinking they might be a couple." Polly shook her head. "Otherwise, why wouldn't Kai just tell you what his relationship with her is?"

"Maybe he didn't want a stranger prying into his business? I mean, on the one hand, I understand it, but on the other hand, it makes it harder to investigate." I continued munching on the popcorn while mulling over the possible significance of Carla and Kai being a couple—or not.

Suddenly, the lights turned off, then a faint blueish light filtered through the curtain.

"Now they're watching TV," Polly groaned. "Maybe we should call it a night."

"Not yet. I'd hate to miss something. Especially if someone leaves the house on foot." I shivered against the cold seeping into the car. Then I finished my bag of popcorn while Polly finished hers.

"You're right—maybe them being a couple has nothing to do with what happened." Polly sank back against the seat and folded her arms.

"You're sure stuck on this couple thing." I glanced over at her. "When was the last time you were in a relationship?"

"Whoa, whoa, whoa. I don't think we need to get personal here. Let's focus on the case." She flipped her collar up and burrowed into her coat.

"Polly." I drew out her name.

"It's not care-and-share time."

"*Polly.*"

She widened her eyes at me. "I'm not here for girl talk." She motioned toward the house. "We're on a mission, in case you forgot."

Said mission was turning out to be a dud, but I didn't want to say so. Instead, I raised my eyebrows at her.

"Oh, fine. It's been a few years."

"How many is a few?"

"Six." Polly pursed her lips and looked away. "Actually, seven."

That was a long time to go without love. My heart softened for my friend. I reached out and squeezed her hand. "What happened? Was he just not marriage material?"

She drew a deep breath, then exhaled, fogging the window. "For your information, he died."

I gasped and covered my mouth—my enormous mouth. "Oh, Polly. I'm so sorry. Forget I said anything."

A faint smile ghosted her lips. "It's okay. Sometimes it's good to remember. And to answer your question, he was absolutely marriage material."

"What happened?" I hesitated to ask, but I still wanted to know.

Polly shook her head. "He died under rather mysterious circumstances. But that's a story for another day." She looked me in the eye. "Let's just say, this investigating stuff…it's not my first rodeo."

Well, that explained the binoculars and whatnot. I made a mental note to ask her again when the time was right.

"What about you and Officer Hotpants?" She peered over at me.

"What about Officer *Hotpants* and me?" I grumbled. "There's nothing to tell. If James hadn't come back to town, we might've made some progress." I pinched my fingers together. "We were this close to a perfect kiss."

"That's not to say you can't pick up where you left off once James is gone."

"*If* he ever gets to leave."

"Pfft. It'll happen." Polly yawned and adjusted her coat. "It's only been a few days. Once we figure out who killed Mason—"

"And get proof."

"And get proof," she affirmed before continuing. "Then he'll pack up and take his man bun back to LA. My guess is that once he's off the hook, he'll be so glad that he'll hightail it out of Beaver Bluff."

I took another sip of soda, hoping for a jolt from the caffeine. "From your mouth to God's ears." Although, if I were completely honest with myself, I secretly enjoyed James's attention. Or maybe his longing for me was vindication for all the havoc he'd wreaked. Yes, that had to be it. I felt a little better after my self-analysis.

The thing no one mentions about stakeouts is how boring they actually are. I leaned against my window, struggling to pay attention. Carla and Kai just *had* to pick tonight for a movie marathon —if that's who was even there.

Eventually, Polly drifted off to sleep. I snuggled deeper into my wool coat and focused on the blueish glow through the curtain. My eyes felt like lead, and I fought against a yawn and lost. Maybe we'd stay just a few more…

A raspy snore jolted me awake.

I sat up, startled. It was two-fifteen. At least two hours had passed. "Polly, wake up." I shook my friend.

She mumbled in a sleepy voice. "Mmm-hmm…you sexy thing…"

"Eww, Polly. Wake. Up." I elbowed her.

"What?" She bolted upright and looked around, her hair mussed on one side. "What'd I miss?"

I looked at Carla's and pointed at the empty driveway. "Oh, man. She's gone!"

THE NEXT DAY at Crumb's, I stumbled through the sleepy line of caffeine-deprived customers, though I doubted any of them were sleepier or more caffeine-deprived than me. Most were on their way to work, but a lucky few were starting their day by meeting with friends for a gab session. That included Naomi and Verity, who chirped entirely too happily with one another over coffee.

Once the line dwindled, I made my way to their table by the window and collapsed in the closest chair. "I have nothing new to report." I left out the part about falling asleep during the stakeout, as it wasn't an important detail.

"That's a shame." Naomi snapped her fingers. "I thought for sure we were onto something big with the whole Kai situation."

Verity's eyes saucered. "Me, too. I can't believe nothing happened." Her innocence convicted me.

"Actually, maybe something did," I confessed.

They both leaned in with expectant gazes. "Well?" they said in unison.

I rubbed my forehead as though it would clear my brain fog. There was only so much I could expect from myself after a restless night. "The truth is…Polly and I…fell asleep."

"Oh, for crying out loud." Naomi palmed her face.

"Why would you do that on a stakeout?" Verity asked.

"Shhh." I glanced around at the other customers. "It was an accident. Also, I didn't see either of you volunteering for stakeout duty, even after we talked about everyone needing to pitch in."

Verity licked the peppermint cinnamon bun frosting off her lips. "You're right. But that still doesn't change the fact we may have missed an important clue."

I sighed. "We were keeping a close eye on the house, even though nothing was happening. It looked like they were watching TV. But after we woke up, the car was no longer in the driveway and the house was dark."

Verity and Naomi groaned in unison. Naomi's lips pursed and parallel tracks formed between her eyebrows. "Where could they have gone so late at night? It may have something to do with the case."

"Or they could've been running to the store," I countered.

They glared at me.

"Fine." I stood, a plan forming in my head. It was quiet enough in the bakery for me to take a short break. "I'm going to get some answers."

"I'm coming too." Verity bolted out of her seat and followed me into the kitchen, where we said goodbye to Lulu and Bert, her assistant. "Where are we going?" she asked when we made it to the alley where we all parked.

"Back to Carla's," I said as we walked outside.

"She might recognize your car. Let's take mine." The car beeped when she clicked the key fob.

I cleared a purse, three books, and a drink off the passenger seat. A few minutes later, we pulled into Carla's driveway. I grabbed the door handle. "I'm going to tell her she needs to pick up her stuff at the B&B."

"Okay, but what if she asks you about chasing down Kai?"

Given my lack of sleep and chippy disposition, I didn't care. "I'll think of something." I exited her car, careful not to let the wind blow the napkins off the floor into the open.

"This I've got to see." Verity climbed out, and together we marched to the front door. "I'm still not sure it's a great idea."

"She has to get her stuff from Dana's place. End of story." I knocked. When there was no answer, I knocked again. "Carla? Are you there? Hello?"

"There's no car in the driveway. Maybe she's not home." Verity craned her neck toward the front window, which was still covered by a curtain.

I pulled out my phone, looked up Carla's Catering, and dialed. Given the quiet state of the neighborhood, it was possible we'd hear the phone ring inside. Instead, we were met with silence.

The call went to voicemail. "Thank you for contacting Carla's

Catering. We are closed this week but will return your call as soon as possible." *Beep.*

I hung up. Suspicions clicked through my foggy brain. Why had I fallen asleep last night? Of all the stupid times to let down my guard. The gang was right to be mad at Polly and me because we had, in fact, missed something important.

"KC, what are you thinking?" Wariness coated Verity's voice.

I shook my head and gritted my teeth. "I have a terrible feeling that Carla pulled a runner."

Chapter Sixteen

AFTER MY SHIFT at Crumb's, I ran back to my house to pack enough fresh clothes to last a couple more days. More than anything, I wanted to crash in my own bed. But of course, James was camped out in front of the television with his feet propped up on the coffee table.

He leaped off the couch, a little too energetically for my current state. "I was hoping to see you today."

I dropped my handbag and keys onto the table in the entryway. "I'm just here to grab a few things."

"But we're alone." He gestured to the empty house. "We could talk. Maybe I could even make you some lunch."

I perked up. "Did you go grocery shopping?"

"No."

"Then you literally can't make me lunch." I moved past him. My mind whirred for excuses to leave him alone without sounding rude, but my tired brain blanked.

James deflated. "I guess I could go hang out down at the bakery. I don't know if you realized this, but there's not a whole lot to do here in Beaver Bluff."

I snorted. "Tell me about it." I went to the kitchen and

plopped down at the table. A giant sigh escaped as fatigue caught up with me.

The chair scraped across the floor when James pulled it out and sat. "Then why do you stay?" His nose wrinkled as he looked around. "You don't have to live like this."

"Hey, now. It's not all bad." Though, as my gaze roved from the shabby furniture to the 1970s refrigerator that would outlive me, I realized I wouldn't mind an upgrade.

"When all this murder stuff is over, come back with me. We can make a fresh start." He reached across the table and clasped my hand.

I jerked away. "I'm happy here."

"You don't look like it."

"That's because I was on a stakeout last night and didn't get any sleep." I gestured at him with both hands. "It was for you…to try to clear your name."

A wide smile broke across James's face. He palmed his chest. "I'm touched. See, you really do care."

"No—I'm doing it so you can go home."

Disappointment flickered in his eyes—eyes that had once captivated me and made me feel safe and loved. He quickly recovered, as he always did. "But, dude, that's still something. Once you get some rest, maybe you'll change your mind."

I leaned back in the chair and yawned. "I won't. At least not now. I've got family and friends, and I'm trying to launch a business." A business that needed attention if I wanted to get it off the ground. A zillion to-do items flashed through my tired brain. "In fact, I should probably do a little work while I'm here."

"I'm cool with that. Then we could go out. There's gotta be at least one good restaurant in this town." His man bun slipped to the side as he scratched his head.

"We are not going out." I enunciated each word. "Which part of this don't you understand?"

James cocked his head to the side and spoke matter-of-factly. "Everyone has to eat. We might as well do it together."

"Stop trying to wear me down." I rubbed my temple.

"Is it working?"

I gritted my teeth. "Fine. Leave me alone for thirty minutes to get some stuff done, and then we can get food. Fast food."

He grimaced. "Babe, you know I'm not crazy about fast food."

"I meant food that is fast!" I snapped.

James held his hands up, then rose from his chair. "I'll just take a little snooze while you work." He backed away toward the bedroom.

Finally alone, I pulled out my tablet and opened the notes app to see what needed to be done first. *Find a cleaner for Dana.* My heart squeezed, thinking about how she'd been left alone to deal with the mess since last Friday. I scanned the internet and found a company in Portland that specialized in biohazards.

Unfortunately, they were booked until Wednesday morning, but that would have to do. I bit my tongue when they gave me a quote, which they made sure I understood could change based on their findings at the scene. Good thing I still had a healthy bank account from when I'd left the big city, but it was dwindling fast. Hopefully, Dana would pay me back sooner rather than later.

I grabbed a cup of coffee before I started on my next few tasks, namely items that had to do with an upcoming fall fiber event for a yarn shop. After finalizing the ad copy to send to the newspaper and uploading photos to their social media channels, I felt a little more on top of my day.

James wandered back into the kitchen.

"Let me just pack up, and we can head out." I shut the cover of my tablet. "I need to stop by the B&B before we eat."

James sucked a big breath through his clenched teeth. "Do we have to? Everyone there thinks I…you know…" He made a skewering motion.

I narrowed my eyes. "If you want to come with me, I'm stopping by the B&B. Take it or leave it."

UNFORTUNATELY, he took it.

When we pulled up in front of the B&B, James flipped the hoodie over his head, pulled the drawstring tight, and then sank lower in the seat. "Try to make it fast, will you?"

I rolled my eyes at him, but I was pretty sure he couldn't see with the hood covering so much of his face and head. I hurried up to the door, not because James asked me to go quickly, but because a cold front had moved in, and I was freezing. One day I would forgo my cute dresses in favor of denim and flannel, but today was not that day.

An eerie stillness circled the old Victorian, and even from the outside, a feeling of doom hung over the property. Maybe I should have called instead, but the thought of not physically checking in on Dana left me unsettled.

A voice from inside the house indicated she was here. I tapped lightly on the door while simultaneously pushing it open. "Hello?" I called into the front room.

Dana stood behind the check-in desk with a cell phone pinned to her ear. "Maybe we can talk later, Phil." She glanced at me. "I have a guest arriving." She hung up and shoved the phone into her pocket. "KC, I didn't expect to see you today."

I fully entered the room and closed the door. The stench of stale food hung in the air, but when I glanced through the front area into the dining room, the catering supplies were gone. "Oh, did Carla come by?"

Dana followed my line of sight. "Yes, thankfully. Though I suppose I still need to air the place out." She offered a slight shrug. "Sorry about the smell."

"Smell? I don't smell anything." I winced inside from the tiny lie, then spoke quickly to cover it up. "When did Carla come by? I tried to get a hold of her to let her know she could, but I never found her."

Dana's forehead puckered. "I don't quite remember. It was

sometime yesterday. To be honest, I can't seem to keep track of anything."

"That's totally understandable. You've been through a lot." I approached her with caution. "I'm just glad that the catering stuff is gone. And I have good news—I've scheduled a special cleaning crew to come take care of…" I glanced toward the death spot.

"Right, right." She visibly relaxed. "I don't know when I'll be able to pay you back."

"It doesn't have to be right away."

Dana cast her gaze to the floor. "It seems you're the only one I don't have to pay back ASAP. And now, with business down, I don't know how I'll catch up."

"I'm sure you'd like to take time off." I studied her face, lined with fatigue. "Maybe you should slow down a little."

She drew a deep breath and stood tall. "Actually, I need to reopen as quickly as possible. It's just that no one wants to stay where a tragedy happened."

"I'm sure that's not true," I said too quickly, even though I knew she was probably right. It was a good thing Verity wasn't here to scold me over the half-truths that so easily slipped out. I set my handbag on the counter. "Hey, I know someone who wants to be here."

"Who?" Hope lit Dana's eyes.

"My friend Naomi. She told me she wanted to book her party at the B&B, but I thought it was too soon. I'll give her a call. I'm sure she'll be excited." My voice sounded too bright to be realistic, but at least in this, I was truthful.

"Are you just saying that to make me feel better?"

"Not at all. In fact, she'd like to have her party at the end of the week." I pulled out my phone and shot a text to Naomi. "It would be a small party, but we want to make it special. Is Friday night okay?"

Dana's gaze roamed toward the dining area, and uncertainty flickered in her eyes.

"If that's too soon, we can totally figure something else out." I tucked my phone away.

She shook her head. "No, Friday would be great." Her voice faltered.

"Oh, goodness." I face-palmed myself. Maybe James was right —I shouldn't have come by. "I'll bet you have a hundred things to take care of. I'm so insensitive."

"I do have arrangements to make, especially now that the coroner has released...the body." She paused to swallow. "But I also have bills, and it would be good for people to see things happening here again."

From a PR standpoint, she was right.

I smiled. "It'll just be a small gathering, and I'll be here to help." I cringed, even as she smiled. It wasn't as though my proverbial plate wasn't already full. And now it was exploding.

SAM'S DINER was situated south of the town square, nestled between a strip mall and the grocery store. Famous for thick burgers and greasy fries, it was a place I rarely went to but craved today for its comfort food. Even though James initially resisted, I offered no alternative.

"Are you sure you can't remember anything else that might be important to the case?" I dragged a fry through a puddle of barbecue sauce.

James glanced around furtively, even though no one else was seated near us. "I already told you, no." He took a huge bite of his bacon double cheeseburger. Apparently, he'd given up on being a vegetarian.

"How did Kai even hear you arguing with Mason? Where were you guys?" I sipped my tea.

"Downstairs in that main room. Other people were hanging out, and it wasn't like I was trying to hide anything." He shrugged and took another bite.

"Who else was there?"

James paused mid-bite and stared out the window. "I think just people working on the house. Contractors, maybe?"

"Any chance one of them was an electrician?" My mind raced back to the day I was there and the electrician stormed out. That person would know exactly how and where to cut the power.

James nodded thoughtfully. "Yeah. I heard him talking about finishing the job, but he'd about had it with Mason."

"And you didn't think that detail was important enough to tell anyone?" I pinched the bridge of my nose, never mind my salty fingers. "Was he there the night of the party?"

"I don't remember seeing him, but that doesn't mean he wasn't there." James tucked into his burger, seemingly unaware of how important this detail could be.

"Can you give me anything to go on? Did you catch his name?" I shoved a fry into my mouth and chomped hard to release tension.

"No. I was too busy being angry with Mason. I was defending you." He reached across the table and covered my hand. "And look, now you're defending me."

It was sweet in its own twisted way. I pulled my hand back. "I can't defend you if you give me nothing to go on. If only I had a name, maybe I could nose around and ask a few questions."

"I didn't catch his name," James said with his mouth full. "But the name on his business van said M&Z Electric."

"Finally, thank you." I wadded up my napkin and threw it onto the plate. "Let's go. I have a lead to follow."

"But I'm not finished." He motioned to his burger.

I wheeled my hand. "Hurry up. This could be the break I've been waiting for."

Minutes later, James and I stood at the register, and he pulled out his wallet.

I angled away from the door where the cold air slithered inside. "Thank you for lunch. I told you you'd like it."

A broad smile lit James's face, and he lifted his eyebrow. "You know I'd do anything for you." He raised his voice. "I love spending time together. It's been a great afternoon, hasn't it?"

"Yes, it actually has." That said, I still couldn't wait to drop him off at my place so I could visit the electrician and see what I could find out. Excitement at following new leads gave me a jolt that even caffeine couldn't match. I tugged James's sleeve. "Let's get going."

A throat cleared behind me. Slowly, I turned.

Hamson stepped aside and motioned toward the door. A strange mixture of irritation and resignation flickered in his dark, brooding eyes. "Pardon me," he said with an icy voice. "I didn't mean to stand in your way."

Chapter Seventeen

BY THE TIME I dropped James off at my house, Polly was calling me, ready for some help with Pooh Bear and Cujo. Though having everyone along would slow me down, I knew she needed a break. My little guys could be a handful, as was confirmed when I walked into her house and saw Cujo trot by with a Manolo Blahnik in his tiny mouth.

"Naughty!" I clapped my hands together, hoping to startle Cujo into dropping my shoe. Instead, he arf-ed and continued on his merry way, his tail wagging behind him. I rolled my luggage into the foyer and looked over at Polly. "I'm too tired to care."

She peered at me over the top of her newspaper. "Hopefully, you're too tired to care about the other shoe he had earlier for breakfast."

I groaned. "Did he at least chew up a full pair? Or were they two different ones?"

She sank below the newspaper, giving me my answer.

I entered the living room and sat next to her on the couch. "You want the good news or the bad news?"

"Always start with the bad because then it can only get better."

"Sage advice." I took a breath before recounting what had just happened. "Hamson saw James and me together at Sam's Diner.

He thought we were together-together. You should've seen the look on his face when we left. It was sad or maybe angry." Actually, I hoped it was unrequited love, but I didn't say so out loud.

"Good! A little jealousy to stir the pot never hurt anyone."

"You can't really believe that." My stomach churned. Whether from the Hamson encounter or from the bacon double cheeseburger, I couldn't be certain.

"Mark my words. He's probably pining over you just as much as you're pining over him." She waggled her eyebrows.

"I don't think anyone's pining, per se." Although I *hoped* Hamson was pining, as Polly suggested.

Pooh Bear meandered over and laid his head on my feet. He looked up at me with so much concern in his eyes that my heart puddled. I reached down and scratched his ears, grateful for my trusty companion. Cujo toddled over and dropped my shoe, then scratched at my legs. "Oh, fine, you little stinker." I scooped him up for a cuddle. I needed all the canine love I could get.

Polly nudged me with her elbow. "Stop brooding and tell me your good news."

I tried to mentally shake off thoughts about Hamson. But all I could see was the angst on his face and the tic of his jaw as I tried to make excuses. He hadn't wanted to hear a word of it, and Officer Leon stood to the side, just shaking her head. James, however, had a triumphant gleam in his eyes until we got back to my house and I booted him out of the car.

"Earth to KC." Polly waved her hand in front of me. "You said you had good news. Is it about the case?"

"Right, sorry." I resituated myself on the couch. "James remembered the name of the electrician who serviced the B&B. I think we need to check it out."

The newspaper crinkled as Polly folded it. "Hot diggity! Although I'm a little surprised that James remembered such a small detail, yet can't tell us who was in the kitchen right before the lights went out."

"I'm surprised too, but it might be the clue we need."

Polly nodded her head thoughtfully. "I remember you saying how mad the electrician was the first time you went to the B&B. I'm not sure how that ties into the night of the murder, but it couldn't hurt to check."

"I figure we could at least fish around. Maybe if I see the man up close, I'll recognize him from the party, or I can match him up with the pictures I took. I got the impression he was some kind of boss or manager since he was upset about taking payment." My head buzzed with excitement, and all thoughts of Hamson vanished for the moment. "The fact that the murder could *not* have happened without the lights going out is important to the case. There were only so many people who could've pulled that part off."

Polly set the crumpled newspaper on the coffee table. "You got that right." She grunted as she pushed herself off the couch. "Well, what are we waiting for?"

We quickly got ready to go. Given the fact Polly thought my sporty ride was too small to accommodate the four of us, we loaded up in her Lincoln Town Car. Riding in the backseat was getting old, but I was too tired to argue with Pooh Bear. Instead, I cuddled Cujo the Manolo Mangler and gave Polly directions to M&Z Electric.

Minutes later, she pulled into the parking lot of a small building next door to the local car dealership. Two white vans with the company's logo sat out front. A man wearing a stiff work shirt and a hat pulled low over his eyes walked out and tipped his chin up to greet us. Then he climbed into the closest van.

"Is that him?" Polly asked. "He certainly looks suspicious. Did you see the way he looked at us?"

I ruffled Cujo's ears while I tried to place him. "No, I don't think he's the one I saw at the B&B, but he does seem familiar." I paused for a moment to scrape my memories for anything relevant but came up empty. "It's probably that I've been focusing on too many faces in all those photos over the last few days."

"I still say he looks suspicious. Then again, a lot of people do,"

Polly admitted as she handed Pooh Bear a dog biscuit. She waited for the man to pull away from the building before speaking again. "So, what are we going to say when we go inside? And what if we don't see the man who was at the B&B?"

"One problem at a time. Let me think…" I nuzzled Cujo while trying to come up with a plausible excuse to march into the building. "Oh, I know—I'll say we need some work done at your house." I set my pup on the floorboard and reached for the door handle.

"Whoa, just hold your honkers. I don't want these guys coming around my place, just in case they had something to do with Mason's death. We don't know who we're dealing with." She met my gaze in the rearview mirror.

"Fine, I'll say I need work at mine." I pictured Verity shooting mental daggers at me for skimming the edges of truth. "I'm sure there's *something* that could be done at my rental, like track lighting. Track lighting would look great in the living room. It's not a total lie."

Polly's face scrunched in the mirror. "I never said it was."

"Oh, right." I opened the car door. "Here goes nothing. Are you coming?"

"After what's been happening with you, I think I'll stay here with the engine running." She shook her head ruefully. "We never know when you'll need a getaway car."

"Good point." I shut the door, then gathered the folds of my dress to keep it from flying up as I approached M&Z Electric. Inside, the front area boasted little besides a counter and a tattered chair. Mail slots were anchored to the wall and had four boxes. I inched closer to read the tiny, printed names.

"Can I help you?" A man stood in the doorway that presumably led to a workroom.

I stood back, startled. It was him, the man with grizzled gray hair, that had stormed out the back door to the B&B the day I'd first met Dana. The embroidered name on his shirt said *Chris*. I caught my breath, then tried to look casual. "Hey there. I need an electrician."

"What kind of work are you looking to have done?" He pulled a pencil from behind his ear and reached for a notepad under the counter. He scribbled unreadable words.

"Track lighting."

Chris looked up from his notes. "Track lighting?"

"Yeah." I twirled a lock of my hair. "I think it would brighten up my living room to enhance the décor. It would give a certain ambiance it's been missing."

Chris sighed and tucked the pencil back behind his ear. "Ma'am, we don't deal in *ambiance*. What you need is a decorator."

He wasn't wrong.

I cleared my throat. "Don't you do all kinds of electrical work? My house is old, so it needs a professional. You can't be too careful."

"That's really not our line of business. We wire new builds and that type of thing."

I quirked my eyebrow. "Just new builds? I was sure I saw you at the Beaver Bluff Bed and Breakfast. That certainly isn't new." Briefly, I wondered if he remembered seeing me that day.

"Big mistake," he said under his breath as he rubbed his head.

"What's that? A mistake?" I slapped my leg and offered a faux chuckle. "That's right—when I saw you, you were pretty upset about not getting paid." I watched his face for a reaction. Then I leaned close and spoke in a conspiratorial tone. "I don't think I'll be getting paid, either."

"Is that so? What do you do for them?" His face showed no sign of recognition.

"Social media and promotions. Of course, after what happened there the other night, they're going to need a lot of help in that area." I silently prayed for him to take the bait.

He snorted as he tucked his notepad back under the counter. "Look, I don't think we're the right people for your track lighting.

We're a commercial operation, and we've got our hands full. I can refer you to a smaller outfit that might get to you sooner."

The business phone rang.

"Hold on a sec." Chris held up a finger to me, then answered. "M&Z Electric…oh hey, yeah…"

I turned away from Chris and pretended not to listen. At the same time, I switched on my phone camera and attempted to angle it toward the mailboxes. If I could just get a shot of the boxes, maybe I'd recognize a name or two, someone who might have an association to last Friday's party. Chris shifted at the same time I snapped the picture. I willed him to move, but he stayed firmly planted, absorbed in his conversation.

"Little punk didn't even show up today. Left us shorthanded." Chris fisted his hand. "I keep trying to call, but it goes to voicemail. Had to reschedule two clients."

Sounded like he was spinning several plates like the rest of us. I gave up trying to take a picture. Maybe track lighting really would be nice, though I didn't want to make an improvement to a rental. Maybe I could get Holly at the property management agency to spring for it.

"In this case, one Fulsom brother is better than two." Chris spat his words. A vein in his neck pulsed, and his face turned red.

I schooled my face to hide my shock. If he wasn't shy about having an outburst in front of a stranger, what else was he capable of? Quickly, I reopened the camera app and started recording, careful to keep it hidden in the crook of my arm.

"I'm telling you, that's it for Kai." Chris pounded the counter with the side of his fist. "The next time I see the little punk, I'm gonna kill him."

Chapter Eighteen

THE LAST THING I wanted after a long day of working and sleuthing was to hit the mats with Verity at the dojo. But it was my only chance to bounce ideas off her with everything I'd learned. After a hearty workout, we bellied up to the makeshift juice bar, which consisted of a long table where we could consume the sports drinks and juice boxes available for purchase.

"I wish you'd called me to come with you and Polly." Verity's gaze swept the floor, and her mouth turned down at the corners.

"Sorry about that. It's just that you haven't been around much lately." I tried to keep the jealousy out of my voice. But I was a little tired of her and David, and Naomi and Walter, pairing off like they were boarding Noah's ark and leaving the rest of us behind.

"Well, I'm here now." She attempted a smile. "Let's hear what happened."

I adjusted myself on the chair to accommodate my aching backside. Our sparring had recently gotten more serious, supposedly because I was improving. Between Verity and Griff, one would think I'd be in stellar shape, but the calories and carbs from Crumb's were winning.

Music played on a speaker overhead in the empty lobby, but I still hesitated to speak openly. I pointed up at the camera mounted in the corner. "Maybe we should wait."

Verity shook her head. "No one's watching right now. Alan's teaching a class."

"Alan?"

"Yeah, the owner." She slurped a homemade smoothie she'd brought with her.

"The one who looks like William Shatner?"

"Who's that?"

"Never mind," I said as I glanced through the window at the class in session. Sure enough, William Shatner's doppelgänger was walking the perimeter while the students rolled around on the mats. I never would understand this sport.

Verity nudged me. "What did you guys find out?"

Quickly, I filled her in on my conversation with Chris, the electrician. Then I pulled up the video of him threatening to kill Kai.

"Whoa." Verity's eyes and mouth rounded. "So first, Chris loses his cool at the B&B with Dana, then he says he's going to kill someone he works with?"

"Not exactly a peaceful guy." I took a swig of the lemon-flavored sports drink I'd purchased from the cooler.

"Maybe it was just an expression." Verity worried her lip, and it was clear she didn't believe that was a real possibility.

"I like that you're always looking for the good in people, but you saw for yourself. He was furious." I rubbed a chill from my arm.

"Wait a sec. Even if he was making a real threat, are we sure he was talking about the same Kai? Carla's Kai?"

I scoffed. "How many Kais do you suppose live in Beaver Bluff? Especially ones connected to this case."

"You're right." Verity sipped thoughtfully for a moment. Then, she lowered her voice as though remembering the sensitivity of our topic. "Are we suspecting Chris now or Kai?"

My lips fluttered when I released a long breath. "Who knows? We have those two, plus Carla. Oh," I said, holding up a finger.

"Let's not forget Randall, the jeweler. The way he warned me to stop asking questions about the murder was kind of scary." I shivered at the memory. "I still think he knows more than he let on." He was one more person I needed to pump for information.

"We need to get back to the crime board and add what we've learned."

I opened a browser on my phone. "Until we can do that, let's take a look at these guys online and see what else we can find out. I'll take Chris, and you take Kai."

"How can I? We don't know his last name." Verity grabbed her phone out of her *The Library Life Chose Me* gym bag. "Maybe I can find some mention of him in connection to Carla." Her thumbs flew over the faceplate. "I just need to come up with her last name, which I'm pretty sure I saw on her website when we were looking before."

"Hold on a minute." I rubbed my forehead. "I think Chris said Kai's last name, but I don't remember the whole conversation."

Verity continued searching, her barely blinking eyes focused on the screen. "Looks like Carla's last name is Reynolds, so now I just need to see if she has any personal social media. That's kind of hard with such a basic name."

"Unless you can find her name in conjunction with Beaver Bluff." I combed my memory for clues in my conversation with Chris. From now on, I'd start recording my interactions with suspects from the moment I walked in the door. That, too, would give me a leg-up on the police, who probably weren't allowed to do that. Once again, I shifted in my seat to ease my aching backside. "I think Chris mentioned a Fulson or Fullman. Maybe Fulsom? I think that was in reference to Kai's last name, but I'm just not positive."

Verity continued working without looking up. "I'll keep trying to find Carla and Kai, and you see what Chris has going on."

I brought up M&Z Electric and poked around on their website. It turned out that Chris was not only the manager but also the owner. His last name was Berman. Unfortunately, he didn't show up on any social channels I was familiar with, which was no surprise. He didn't strike me as the type to friend and like other people. There were, however, several mentions of his business both on Facebook and in Yelp reviews. A few of them mentioned both the fabulous quality of his work and his unpleasant demeanor.

Then, I pulled up the gallery on my phone to have another look at the pictures from Friday night's soiree. Chris didn't appear in any of the photos, which made sense. There would have been no reason for him to be there. But that didn't mean he didn't come inside through the kitchen and cut the lights at an opportune time.

"You were right." Verity finally looked up from her phone. "His last name is Fulsom."

I leaned over to peruse her findings. "How'd you track him down?"

"Through Carla, like we thought. She was all over Facebook with public posts until two days ago, and now poof…she's gone silent."

"That's really suspicious." I scooted my chair closer to get a better look. "Then where did Kai come in?"

"He was in a few of her posts, and it looks like they're roommates, nothing more. At least according to the public posts." She enlarged a picture of the two of them toasting each other at a birthday party. The caption suggested they were the *best roomies ever*.

"And what about his profile?"

"Not much to look at, really. But I haven't checked other social channels where someone under thirty might be more active." Verity's phone buzzed with a text. She opened it and grinned, then her thumbs went to work again, answering. "Sorry, but I have to bug out."

"Let me guess—David."

She broke into a dreamy smile. "C'mon, we made some progress on the case. Let's be happy about that."

"I guess so." I tucked my phone into my gym bag. "Maybe I'll check out Kai's other social media when I get home…since I don't have anyone waiting for me." Well, maybe Pooh Bear and Cujo were. That thought brought a little comfort.

"Aww, I'm sorry about what happened." Verity cuffed my shoulder. "I'm sure you and Hamson will patch things up."

While we'd been working out, I'd told Verity what happened at the diner. I still felt unsettled about the situation, but there wasn't much I could do. I had to solve the case so I could get rid of James. Nothing less would fix the problem. I went through a mental checklist of steps I could take to move things along.

An idea flickered in my mind. I pulled my phone back out and opened another browser. "I'm going to contact Carla by responding to the newsletter she sent the other day when I signed up. She's either guilty or she knows something, otherwise, she wouldn't have disappeared."

"There's a real email address on the other side of her newsletter?"

"Yeah, as far as I know. She had it set up as an auto-response, but if I reply to it, I'm sure she'll see it." I put Carla's name in my email search bar.

"What are you going to say?"

I started typing, reading it aloud to Verity at the same time. "I know you're hiding."

THE WHOLE HAMSON deal still bugged me, so instead of heading back to Polly's place, I turned left out of the parking lot and drove east of downtown. I entered the quiet residential area where the houses were nicely spaced, and the trees cushioned the night sounds of Beaver Bluff.

When I eased the car to a stop at the curb, I second-guessed my decision to come here. Naturally, it was a bad idea, but the tug on my heart overruled my weary brain. I climbed out of my car and mounted the steps, wondering how Hamson was able to keep his giant pots of flowers alive this time of year. They had to be fake, but at least he kept a nice home.

The door opened before I knocked. "Oh, hi." I tripped over my words.

Hamson's sturdy form filled the doorway, and the light from the living room cast him in a shadow that made his expression unreadable. "Look, if you're here to talk about what happened today, just don't."

Of course, I was here to talk about what happened today, but I wasn't going to lead with that. I chuckled softly and waved off his comment. "I came here because…to tell you what I'd recently learned. It could be important to the case."

With one arm holding the door and one hand shoved in the pocket of his jeans, he held his position.

"Can I come in? It's a little cold." My workout leggings were no match for the late-autumn breeze.

His defeated sigh offered no hope. But he stepped aside and swept his hand to usher me into the house. "This is a bad idea."

You're telling me.

"Do you want to hear what I found out or not?" My gaze traveled the living area, decorated with rustic fabrics and dark, masculine colors. A couch, a loveseat, and an easy chair circled a stone fireplace where low embers crackled, winding down for the night. "Nice place. You have a real eye for—"

"KC," he softly interrupted. "Why are you here?"

I spoke as I crossed the room to the loveseat. "Like I said, I have news about the case."

"You could've called the station." The door clicked shut. Hamson took cautious strides toward me. His Henley shirt stretched taut across his chest, but I forced myself not to look. At least not too much.

I sat firmly to one side of the loveseat and silently willed him to join me. Instead, he took a spot on the couch and angled my way. I shifted back to the middle. "It's not that I don't trust the others, but let's face it, they didn't do a great job with the last two investigations. Well, we know why the first one didn't go well, but still."

With a tilt of his head, he ceded the point. "What did you find out? Just tell me, and I'll pass it along if I think it's relevant." Warm light from the fire danced in his dark eyes, and the softness of his expression belied his professional tone.

I quickly sifted through all the points Verity and I had just discussed to pick one. "Carla and Kai both fled. They're gone."

"How would you know this?"

I drew a thankful breath. At least he was listening. "I've tried and tried to find Carla, and she's just disappeared. And I went to the place Kai works, and man, his boss is furious at him for taking off without a trace."

It took half a second for Hamson's expression to morph from soft to irate. "You went to Kai's *work*?"

"Settle down." I opened the gallery on my phone. "I'll show you the video. It may even be Chris that's guilty. You should see—"

"You took *video*?" His volume cranked higher.

Just then, Hamson's tuxedo cat named Figaro strode into the room and meowed. Apparently, he needed to see for himself if his person was okay.

"Shhh. You're upsetting Figgy." I reached out my hand, and Figaro sauntered over for a scratch. "We don't need to get so angry now, do we, Figgy?"

Hamson bolted off the couch and raked his hand through his hair. "You can't just take video of people."

I shook my head and pulled Figaro to my lap. He'd grown even bulkier since the last time I'd seen him—if that was even possible. "You mean, *you* can't just take video of people. I'm a private citizen in a public place, so the same rules don't apply."

Hamson paced in front of the fire. "I'm pretty sure it's a private business, and the rules…you know what, never mind." He growled unintelligible words as he fisted his hands on his waist.

"Do you want to see the video or not?" I waved my phone at him.

"No, I don't." His broad shoulders heaved with a breath. Then he spoke with remorse. "You need to stay out of the investigation. Remember what happened to you last time?" His neck bobbed with a hard swallow. "You're putting yourself and your friends in danger."

I winced, knowing he was right but unable to stop myself. I set the cat down and approached Hamson too quickly, causing him to take a step back. "Don't you see? The only way for me to get rid of James—who, by the way, I have no feelings for—is to figure out who killed Mason."

Hamson started to pace again, and I followed in his wake. Figaro followed us both.

I continued with my pleas. "Unlike Carla and Kai, James didn't run. He's innocent, but he's not going to leave until your people say he can go. And believe me," I slid my finger down Hamson's arm. "I want him gone."

Hamson closed his eyes and shook his head almost imperceptibly. Then he ushered me to the front door and rested his hand on the handle. "I need you to stay out of it and stay safe."

I edged closer and drew in his musky scent. "Your concern is *really* nice." I positioned myself in the small space between Hamson and the door.

He leaned in, trapping me between his arm and the wall. "I don't know how to make it any clearer. Stay away from the suspects." His gaze met mine, and his breath swept across my face. "At least one of them is dangerous." The low rumble of his voice vibrated through me.

"Probably more than one," I whispered.

Hamson began to close the gap between us, then paused with his lips mere inches from mine. Desire flamed in his eyes, but he abruptly pulled back and shook his head. Then he opened the door, letting a cold gust inside. "I told you this was a bad idea."

Quite the contrary. Seeing Antonio alone was probably the

best idea I'd had in a very long time.

Chapter Nineteen

CARLA STILL HADN'T RESPONDED by the next day when I went to work at Crumb's. Thoughts about the case were more than a little distracting as I served up coffee and pastries (and sampled some, as well).

As soon as the line of Tuesday regulars dwindled to one that Krystal could manage on her own, I slipped into the back so I could check for any new messages. Cinnamon and vanilla laced the air and the scent of peppermint from the cinnamon rolls on the menu as the holidays approached.

Aunt Lulu switched off the industrial-sized mixer. "What's going on with you? You seem distracted today."

"I think I did pretty well, all things considered." *All things* being a murder case to solve and another near kiss with Hamson. Anyone would botch a few orders under those circumstances.

"Is something happening with the case?" Lulu swiped flour from her cheeks.

"Yes and no." I breezed past Lulu and headed for the break-room. I peeled off my apron, slung it over the hook, and then grabbed my handbag. "We should have another meeting tonight to catch everyone up and see what the others may have found," I said when I came back into the kitchen.

"Just say the word, and I'll be there."

My phone buzzed. I pulled it out of my bag. "It's Dana from the B&B. I'd better take this." I kissed Lulu's cheek, then answered the call as I stepped out the back door. "Hey, what's up? Is everything okay?"

"Didn't you tell me that the cleaning company would be here on Wednesday?" A thread of panic laced Dana's voice.

"Yes. Did something happen? Did they cancel?" My car chirped when I unlocked it. I slid behind the wheel.

"No. In fact, they showed up today, but I have someplace I'm supposed to be." Her voice wobbled. "I need your help."

"Hang on. I'll be right there." I backed out of my space and headed for the B&B.

Minutes later, I pulled in behind a van with a sign that boasted their biohazard cleanup business. I hurried up the walkway and entered the B&B. A three-person crew in head-to-toe gear worked in the dining area, one removing fingerprint powder and two working on the death spot.

"Dana, are you here?" I called.

"I think she's out back." One cleaner pointed toward the swinging door to the kitchen.

I thanked them as I carefully skirted the death spot. Then I cautiously opened the swinging door. "Dana? I'm here." The empty kitchen still bore the marks of the investigation. I let the door swing shut behind me. "Hello?"

The soft murmurs of the cleaning crew sounded through the door, but the kitchen remained silent. I glanced to the right, toward the hall leading to the storage room. According to James's story, that's where the back door was. Slowly, I walked in that direction, my eyes fixed on the breaker box, presumably where the murderer would have cut the power—a murderer James never saw.

"Dana?" I called softly as I made it to the short hallway, noting the fingerprint powder covering the breaker box. Where would the murderer have hidden? I continued past the hall and into the storage room.

And there it was. A nook opened right behind the wall where the hallway ended. It was a space big enough for a grown person to hide, as long as no one turned their head upon entering the storage room to look.

James would have been too flustered and upset after a confrontation with Mason to glance behind him into the nook. And it would've taken whoever was there about two seconds to slip out of the hiding space and cut the power.

Dana's muffled voice sounded outside the back door. "Not going to work…told you…"

I crept past two washers, two dryers, and a long counter. While I didn't want to invade her privacy, I couldn't resist. I stood near an entryway, opposite a narrow staircase, which would have been the one James went up after Mason told him to leave.

"Yes, Phil. Love…talk soon." The back door squeaked.

I hopped away from my secluded position and pretended to have been walking the whole time. "Just coming to find you."

Dana shoved her phone inside her pocket. She swiped a tear from her eye. "Sorry, I'm such a mess."

"No problem. I'm here to help." I palmed my chest. "Whatever you need."

She wiped more tears with the collar of her flannel shirt. "I'm falling apart, and I just can't handle…" she hiccupped. "Any of this. It's…overwhelming."

I rubbed her back and ushered her further inside. "I can only imagine. What is it I can help you with? Do you need me to supervise the cleaners while you get some rest?"

She shook her head vigorously. "No, that's the easy part."

In that case, I didn't want to know what the hard part was. But like it or not, I was here for the long haul. "What is it then? What can I do?"

"I was supposed to take Mason's suit over to the…" Her shoulders heaved with a sob. Then she paused to catch her breath before she spoke. "Mortuary. They're ready to dress him as soon as the…funeral director gets there today."

"Okay." I drew out the word, unsure where she was going with this.

She looked at me with teary eyes. "Can you take it over? They're expecting me any minute, and I just can't bear it."

"I…uh…" I hated to say no. While I had many skills, funeral arrangements were outside my areas of expertise.

"You don't have to arrange anything," she hastened to say, reading my mind. "At this point, all they need is…Mason's clothes," she sniffled.

I cringed inside but mustered a hopeful smile. "Absolutely. I'm on it."

SINCE VERITY TOLD me she wanted to be more involved, I dragged her to the funeral home. No way did I want to go alone, even to drop off Mason's suit.

"Honestly, this isn't a big deal," Verity said as we ascended the steps leading into the mortuary. "Just drop off his clothing and get back to what you were doing."

"You mean you want to get back to what *you* were doing." I shot her a pointed glare, as I had, in fact, pulled her away from cuddling up with David at Yum Yum's Ice Cream downtown. "I'll take you back when we're finished." I slung the plastic-covered suit over my arm.

Verity rolled her eyes, then opened the front door.

Soft music played inside. The sound of a man crying came from a room off to the side of the lobby. Then a woman chimed in with tears. Though I wasn't an expert in funerals, the extensive sobs seemed a little over the top, but who was I to say?

The floor in the aging house-cum-mortuary creaked as we crossed the entrance. To one side of the waiting area was a sectioned-off room filled with chairs, presumably to hold services.

A door was propped open to the side of that room, but that didn't seem to be where the crying was coming from. More sobs indicated the bereaved were adjacent to the waiting area. Then, a terse voice cut over the crying, warning them to settle down.

Verity wrinkled her nose. "Maybe we should leave the suit here."

"But how will they know it belongs to Mason?" I craned my neck to see if anyone was coming to help us.

"We'll leave a note." She nodded her head toward the crying. "It seems rude to interrupt."

I readjusted Mason's suit to keep the plastic from sliding off my arm. "We're not interrupting. We'll just wait until someone comes out."

But the longer we waited, the less likely it seemed that someone would notice our presence, until finally, a harried woman with frowsy brown hair and a nametag that said Lisa appeared. She startled when she saw us. "I'm so sorry," she said as she clutched her chest. "I didn't know you were here."

"That's okay. I totally understand." I glanced at the room where the crying had given way to abrupt voices, then lowered my voice to a reverent tone. "I just came by to drop off Mason's suit."

A stern voice spoke in the background. "Well, if you'd cared that much for him in life, maybe his death wouldn't be hitting you this hard."

Verity and I gasped.

Lisa grimaced. "Yes, we were expecting you, Dana—"

"No, no," I said.

"You can just leave this with me." The plastic rumpled when Lisa reached for the suit. "As you can see, the funeral director is out, and I'm the only one here." She motioned over her shoulder toward the cacophony. "So sorry, but I need to get back."

"That's fine. Do what you need to." I offered a flimsy smile.

The woman marched toward the consultation room, then she abruptly spun around. "Oh, one thing…do you want his viewing to be with his…" She motioned to her face.

"What?" I looked between the woman and Verity, trying to make sense of the question.

The mortuary worker glanced over her shoulder, then back at me. "With or without?" Once again, she motioned to her face, her eyes pleading for me to understand.

"With," Verity cut in.

Lisa nodded, turned, and hustled back into the ruckus. She shut the door firmly, and the muffled voices turned back into crying ones.

"I don't understand what she's talking about. 'With' what?" I asked in a hushed tone.

Verity shrugged. "Who knows? Let's get out of here. These are some seriously bad vibes."

A thought occurred to me, something that had niggled at me from the first time I'd met Mason. I caught Verity by the arm. "Keep a lookout." I glanced between the consultation room and the propped-open door to the back of the viewing area. "I wonder if he's in there."

"Who?"

"Mason." I tiptoed toward the viewing room.

"You can't go in there." Verity tried to catch my arm, but I eluded her grip.

"Says who? No one else is here." I scurried down the aisle between the chairs, throwing cautious glances over my shoulder for any signs of Lisa or anyone else. Thankfully, she was occupied with the brawling bereaved.

Verity hesitated but followed in my wake. "This is going too far." She stage-whispered so loudly I was surprised no one else had heard. Still, it didn't stop me. I'd just have to be quick.

Cautiously, I pushed against the door. "Hello?" I said, just in case someone was inside. I could always make up a reason I was there if I needed to. "Hello?"

No answer. The room itself was casketed in silence, away from the music and the crying.

The door protested as I pushed it open just wide enough for

me to poke my head inside. Clearly, this was not an embalming room or any place where they did all their secret mortuary stuff. Instead, the room was decorated more like a bedroom, from the wallpaper to the dressers. Volumes of books with aging spines rested near another door. And there, on the far side of the room, was what I was looking for.

A table leaned against the wall, holding a solid form underneath a sheet.

My breath caught in my throat, and I hesitated before crossing the threshold. I had to at least take a peek, or I wouldn't be able to confirm my suspicions one way or another.

"KC, hurry up." Verity's words drifted in from outside the door. "I think someone's coming. I saw a car pull up."

I waved her off, even though I knew she couldn't see me, then carefully approached the table while holding my breath. My eyes rounded, and I stifled a gasp. My heart jumped into overdrive as I pondered the implications. This would send the investigation in a whole different direction.

I didn't even have to lift the sheet to know it was Mason underneath because resting on a stand near a giant makeup case sat his bristly, walrus-like mustache.

Chapter Twenty

"QUICK, SOMEONE'S HERE." Verity's stage-whisper was enough to wake the dead.

I hustled over to the door. But as I tried to come out, Verity pushed me back inside just as I caught sight of a man wearing a nametag. "Crap," I muttered.

"What do we do?" she whispered frantically.

"Hey," the man called from the lobby. "You can't be in there."

Verity and I looked at one another, panic-stricken. I pointed to the other door, nearer to Mason's body. We dashed towards it, and I prayed it would open. Footsteps sounded from the viewing room behind us. The mortuary worker angry-whispered, as though he was trying to be reverent and trying to stop us at the same time.

"Hurry." She shoved me from behind, then suddenly, she stopped. "What on earth—"

"Yes, it's his mustache." I yanked her sleeve with one hand, and with the other, I jerked open the door, which led to a kitchen.

My heeled boots tapped against the tile floor, and Verity's work boots sounded behind me as we passed a table holding the remnants of a veggie pizza.

A panic-laced shriek edged up my throat as the suited man

entered the kitchen. My heart lurched inside my chest, but adrenaline propelled me toward the far side of the room.

"This is trespassing!" The mortuary worker was mere steps behind us.

"Sorry!" Verity called out as she shoved me out the back door and into a sideyard.

Icy wind slapped my face the moment we made it outside. Together, we rounded the corner of the mortuary and bolted toward my car. I reached for my key fob and clicked the button once, twice, three times to ensure it was unlocked.

Verity and I slid inside the car, and I reversed out of the space before I even closed the door.

"Go, go, go!" she screamed.

"I am!" I threw the car into drive, cranked the wheel, and gunned the gas.

In the rearview mirror, the suited man jumped up and down, waving his arms. Finally, he threw up his hands as Verity and I peeled out of the lot.

I clutched my chest, willing my heart to dial down a few notches. "That was a close call. You know, we could've just told him we got lost. Or that we wanted to see Mason one last time."

Verity rolled down her window. Her red hair blew wildly around her face as she spoke over the music blaring through the speakers. "But this way, we didn't have to lie. We shouldn't have been in there."

I slid my sunglasses on. "If they really wanted to keep people out, they would've locked the door. Besides, it wasn't like an embalming room or anything. More like a staging area," I reasoned.

"What was up with that mustache?" Verity swiped hair out of her eyes.

"Right?" I turned off the music so I could process my thoughts. "The thing is, why did Mason want to disguise himself? What was the point of hiding his face?"

"I think that *was* the point."

"But why?" Suspicions crowded my thoughts about Mason's false mustache and drab khaki clothing. My hands still shook from the adrenaline rush. "I think we've been going at this all wrong. It's Mason we should've been investigating."

ACCORDING TO VERITY, the library is the best place to do research, which was where we found ourselves minutes later. She grabbed a laptop from behind the reference desk and met me in a study room where we'd have some privacy.

"I'm going to log in as an employee, then I'll have access to the paid databases." Verity booted up while I opened my trusty tablet.

"I always felt like something was off with Mason. I mean, besides his creepy leering." The memory of his eyes flicking over me caused me to shudder. Even death didn't excuse that behavior. As mad as I was at James, it really was sweet of him to stick up for me.

Verity cracked her knuckles. "Okay, let's see what we can find out about Mason Dunn." With impressive speed, her fingers flew over the keys.

Meanwhile, I started going through various social media sites to see what kind of footprint Mason had created for himself. After several minutes, I shook my head. "He's another one of those people who doesn't have any social media—at least not that I can find."

"Not everyone likes to spread their business all over the internet." Verity spoke without her fingers breaking stride.

"But at least some social sites are necessary just for everyday life." I opened a fresh diet soda and took a sip. The bubbles soothed me as I continued to ponder. "That's why people sometimes use variations of their names to put on different sites, if only to join groups and whatnot to receive basic information. Maybe

I'll see what Dana has and if she's connected to anyone with a variation of Mason's name."

Verity stopped typing. "I know you find it hard to believe, but some people really live without being online at all. I see it every day in the library—people who need help just getting onto a computer for a basic search. Maybe Mason was one of those people."

"Which was probably why he was leery about me helping set up their social media." I capped my bottle.

"Unless," Verity said as she resumed typing. "Mason isn't his name at all."

"What do you mean?" I looked over her shoulder, unsure what I was looking at.

"I'm not finding any trace of a Mason Dunn in this area." She pointed to the screen. "There should at least be a business license or something. I'll check under Dana's name next."

For the next several minutes, Verity and I started searching online for Dana. There was more to her, but not much. I nudged Verity. "Here's a profile for her, but it only goes back about a year. And she only has three posts, one of which was the day they opened the B&B. I'll bet most of her posts are set to private." I hated when people did that. It made my job much harder.

"This is so not cool." Verity looked up from the laptop. "I'm not finding a whole lot about either of them. It's like they've scrubbed themselves from the internet."

"That's what I was trying to say," I gestured to my tablet. "It's just not normal."

Verity shook her head. "Not finding traces of them online is different from them not being on social media. Basically, everything we do in life leaves some type of electronic footprint—especially if you know where to look."

I closed the cover of my tablet and sat back. None of this was adding up as it should, but I wasn't sure why. Maybe if I could get a good night's sleep, some pieces would start falling into place.

There had to be a reason this brother and sister duo had no electronic footprint. But what?

Verity's voice cut through the silence. "Are you thinking what I'm thinking?"

"That Mason's mustache was more than just a poor fashion choice?"

She huffed. "Obviously. But what I'm getting at is, Mason might not be his name at all. What if they have fake identities?"

I drummed my fingers on the desk. "Mason, sure. But not Dana. All I can see is her sad eyes and rumpled clothes and…nope."

Verity scoffed. "She has you snowed."

"What? No way."

"Then why can't we find anything about her from the past?" Verity tilted her head and blinked rapidly, her expression daring me to dispute the facts. "I've done a million searches on people, and I can usually turn up *something*."

"Great, then how are we going to find out who they are—*if* you're even right."

Verity slouched against her metal chair. "I guess we could hire a detective."

"*We* are the detectives." I motioned back and forth between us. "Besides, I've spent a crap-ton of money for a cleaning crew because I felt sorry for Dana. She has to be who she says she is. Got any other bright ideas?"

We sat in silence, mulling over the situation. Then, we quietly resumed our searching.

Finally, a thought occurred to me. "What about an image search? If they have an online presence with their real identities, then we could find out what's in their past. Their past has to be the key to this whole thing." However, I still refused to believe Dana had been lying.

"It would only work if we could get a picture of Mason without his mustache."

"Fine," I said as I stood.

"Where are we going?"

I stuffed my tablet into my handbag. "Back to the mortuary so I can get a picture of Mason without a mustache."

"Eww, no!" Verity's eyes bugged out.

"Shhh." I held my finger to my lips. "We're in a library."

RATHER THAN HEADING BACK to the funeral home, Verity talked me into trying the B&B first. A white van from M&Z Electric sat at the curb when we pulled up. I eased in from behind and sandwiched that van between my car and the biohazard vehicle.

"Maybe there's a picture of Mason on the wall or something." Verity's hopeful tone made me reluctant to burst her bubble, but I seriously doubted it. At least not a picture without his mustache, if he were really trying to conceal his identity.

"We'll figure something out. At least we can tell Dana that we dropped off the suit." I grabbed my handbag before exiting the car.

The front yard appeared much more cheerful than it had recently. Someone had taken the time to clean up the remaining debris from last week's party. As we headed up the walkway, a man wearing a hat from M&Z stepped onto the porch and headed down the stairs.

The electrician hitched his chin at us. "Hey, how you doing?" It was a greeting, not a question.

I nodded. "Doing great." Aside from a brush with the mortician, what I told him was true. When he was out of earshot, I turned to Verity and whispered. "That's the guy I saw yesterday. I wonder if he knows anything about Kai since they're coworkers? Maybe I should go ask."

Verity caught my arm. "Let's focus on one task at a time. We need a picture of Mason, unless you can think of a way to look for him without doing a reverse image search."

The porch creaked as we crossed it. "I guess we could come

out and ask Dana why we can't find any trace of them before a year ago." I shrugged. "Isn't that what you prefer, the totally honest approach?"

Verity's green eyes slivered. "Very funny. I like to be honest, not stupid." She pushed open the door. "After you."

The quiet drone of people working in tandem to clean the B&B drifted through the air, though it was clear they'd moved on to the kitchen. I shut the door behind us just as Dana appeared from the hallway that led to the office in the turret.

"You came back." Surprise lit her tired face. "How did it go?"

Verity and I looked at each other. I stepped toward Dana. "There was a bit of a commotion while we were there, so we didn't really get to talk."

Who knew there could be so much arguing over funeral arrangements? The few I'd been to had been simple, lovely gatherings with songs and flowers and pictures of the dearly departed…which gave me an idea.

"Dana, what about photos of Mason…for the service?" I watched her face for traces of hesitation.

She hesitated. "I don't think that will be necessary. It's going to be a small gathering."

I moved towards her. "But it can still be meaningful. We can help you pick just the right one to put up at the entrance, and then another one for the program, and of course, we'll need one for the obituary." Why hadn't I thought of that before? Gathering information for the obit would be a great way to discover Mason's history and see if said history was entirely made up.

"Obituary?" Dana's mouth crimped. "I don't think he'd want that."

Not if he was hiding his identity. I forged ahead. "We'll still need one for the program and several for the picture board."

"Picture board?" Dana echoed.

"Some families have them set up at the chapel entrance, so loved ones can remember the good times," I spoke as though I actually knew something about funerals. But really, what was a funeral but an end-of-life party? And I was great at throwing parties. "When it's over, you can have the picture board as a keepsake."

"I could help you put one together." Verity volunteered.

Hopefully, she would make one without the bubble font she was so fond of using for our crime boards. I offered a sad smile to match Dana's. "All we need are some pictures to get us started."

"Have a seat." Dana gestured toward a couch in the sitting area near the window. Moments later, she returned from the office with a handful of pictures, including one in a small frame. "I don't have many." She sat in the small space between Verity and me, then sifted through the first few.

Verity and I made appropriate cooing noises over each picture that she showed, all of which had Mason with a mustache and appeared to have the B&B in the background. We needed one that was older.

"Ma'am?" One of the biohazard cleaners poked their head out of the swinging door to the kitchen. "Can I have a quick word?"

Dana sighed and handed me the small stack of pictures. "Duty calls."

"Take your time," Verity said.

As soon as Dana pressed through the swinging door, Verity and I rummaged quickly through the stack. Only two photos featured Mason without a mustache. The framed one looked like it came from the turn of the century, and one of them posing together at the beach.

"Quick, get a shot of these." Verity angled the pictures toward me.

I whipped out my phone and snapped several times, hoping to get one clear enough to use on a reverse image search to help us find Mason with his picture instead of his name. "Here, put them back in order."

"Unfortunately, I think I committed to making a picture board for his funeral." Verity's face twisted. "Maybe she'll let me keep these, in which case we didn't really need to take pictures of the pictures."

Just then, Dana emerged from the kitchen. I tucked my phone under my bottom. "I think we've got what we need."

"Let me just see." She quick-stepped towards us and held out her hand. Then she sorted through the stack and held back the ones without the walrus-like mustache. "Thank you two for your help. You have no idea what this means to me." She sniffed and held her hand to her face. "We came here for a fresh start. And I was almost happy."

"Come again?" I asked, hoping she'd elaborate.

Dana shook her head. "Nothing." She glanced over her shoulder. "I need to get back to work. I have to get the B&B in shape for business again. Thanks for coming by."

Cool, refreshing ocean air greeted Verity and me as we walked outside the B&B. Fortunately, the electrician had been able to squeeze out from between my car and the biohazard people's.

"Mission accomplished." I held up my phone as we meandered down the path toward the curb. "Let's head around the corner to Polly's, and we can do the reverse image search."

Verity stopped short. "Uh, I don't think we'll be going anywhere." She pointed to my car, where the front passenger side tire lay flat on the pavement...with a stainless-steel shish kebab skewer rammed into the sidewall.

<h1 style="text-align:center">Chapter Twenty-One</h1>

THE SECOND AUNT Lulu flipped the sign from opened to closed, the gang started buzzing all at once, asking for updates about the slashed tire. Even Pooh Bear and Cujo crooned from their position under the table closest to the door.

"Are you guys doing that investigating thing again?" Krystal's face scrunched with disapproval.

We all stopped talking.

"You can go on home." Lulu ushered Krystal toward the kitchen. "We'll do the cleanup. Enjoy your afternoon off."

"But I need the hours—"

"And I'll pay you." Lulu flicked a hand towel toward Krystal as she disappeared behind the swinging door. "See you in the morning!"

The buzz resumed, the ladies flinging questions at Verity and me all at once. I grabbed a peppermint scone to nibble on while I waited for them to get it all out of their system. As much as the skewer in the tire had shaken me too, I was mostly excited about the fact that we were on the right trail. Too bad we didn't know which one it was.

Lulu stood over me with her hands fisted on her hips. "Did you at least call the police?"

"No!" Verity and I answer together. Instead of calling the police, I'd texted the picture to Carla, hoping to flush her out of hiding. Even if she wasn't the one who slashed my tire, it sure looked like her calling card.

"Then we would have had to admit we were investigating on our own." Verity looked at each one of us solemnly. "And you know how they feel about that."

"But this has gone too far." Lulu collapsed in the chair next to mine and rubbed her head. "Clearly, someone is warning you to back off."

"What else is new?" I took another delicious bite and savored the hint of peppermint. "At least this time, I didn't end up in the hospital."

"Yet!" Lulu butted in. "You haven't ended up in the hospital *yet*." Pooh Bear meandered over and slid his head under her hand for comfort. Cujo trailed behind him and yipped his support.

"All it means is that we're getting close to figuring out who killed Mason." I dusted my hands over the table, feigning more confidence than I felt. "It'll be okay. Let's just stick to our original plan and go out in pairs. We'll be safe."

Naomi pulled a tissue out of her brassiere and dabbed her eyes. "I can't help but worry. What if you'd come out of the B&B and saw that person? What would they have done to you?"

"Nothing," I said firmly. "Clearly, that person doesn't want to confront us face-to-face."

Verity's eyes narrowed. "She's right. It was a cowardly move. I dare them to come get a piece of this action." She wheeled her hands around, ready to fight.

"Oh, brother." Polly, silent up to this point, rolled her eyes. Secretly, I was certain she was a little jealous that Verity had been with me instead of her. It was probably better that way, though, or Polly would've been shouting for the perp to come out of hiding.

"Take us through this afternoon, and don't leave anything out." Lulu twined her fingers together as though bracing herself.

Verity and I recounted the day from the time we picked up

Mason's suit at the B&B, to seeing his mustache and being chased out of the mortuary. We ended with our ruse to get a picture of him and my tire getting punctured. The only bit we left out was texting the picture to Carla, accusing her of the crime. There was no use in getting the gang more worked up than they already were.

"I knew there was something phony about that man." Polly sipped her coffee. "I just didn't realize it was the mustache, but it all makes sense. He wanted to conceal his identity. The question is, why?"

"If only we could get his real name." Naomi licked the tip of her finger and dotted the crumbs on her plate.

"We can," I said as I pulled out my tablet. "That's why Verity and I got an old picture of him—so we could do a reverse image search. That's where you load an image and search for matches online, rather than searching with words."

"They aren't always reliable, but without marching up to Dana and asking why there's no trace of her or her brother's past online, this is the best option. Let's do it now while we have everyone here." Verity pointed to my tablet.

"First, I need to send the pictures to my tablet." I made a few swipes on my phone and waited for the images to go through.

"Are you thinking that his former identity—if it turns out that Mason has one—is the reason he was killed?" Lulu leaned over to look at my tablet.

"It may have nothing to do with the murder." I pulled up the reverse images site. "But it seems awfully suspicious."

Naomi's eyes rounded. "Oh, I wonder if he's running from bad guys, and they finally caught up to him."

"Or if he *is* one of the bad guys," Polly said.

"Here goes nothing." I loaded the first photo, the oldest one from the frame. Seconds ticked on and on. Stupid wi-fi. Finally, the results populated as everyone gathered around and looked over my shoulder.

"Why is it showing gold chains as possible matches?" Naomi's fluffy white hair ruffled as she shook her head. "I don't think it's working right."

"Narrow down the field to just his face," Verity instructed.

Polly snorted. "Speaking of which, I can see why he chose to cover it with that mustache."

We groaned in unison.

"What?" She held up her hands defensively. "You know you were thinking it."

"The only thing I'm thinking about is the case. We need to figure this out so I can send James packing." I looked at each of my friends for emphasis, as if they didn't already know.

"Try again." Verity pointed to the screen.

I narrowed the scope of the search to Mason's face and hit the search button. Slowly, images populated the screen—this time with pictures of people. Too bad none of those people were Mason, as most of them were women. "I'm going to try the other picture and see if we have better luck."

Everyone sat back in their chairs, dispirited from the first set of results. Only Verity remained.

After loading the second picture and pressing the search button, more images loaded. At least this time, they were men. I scrolled past the obvious mismatches.

"Keep going," Verity said. "Sometimes, you find what you want in the last place you look."

"Uh…isn't that always the case?" Polly gestured. "Once you find something, you stop looking. Therefore, it was the last place you looked."

"She has a point." Naomi nodded matter-of-factly.

"I'm trying to say that we keep searching until we find what we're looking for without giving up too soon." Exasperation punctuated Verity's words.

Moments later, I pointed to the screen. "And this is why we don't give up."

Everyone gathered around me and oohed.

"Are we sure this is him?" Lulu glanced between us all.

"You can't get a closer match than the exact same picture." Verity pointed between the picture I loaded and the one from a newspaper headline.

"That sure explains a lot," Polly said.

Naomi stood on her toes and tried to peer between Verity and Lulu. "I can't see. Someone read it to me."

I tapped on the picture to open the article. "The headline says, 'Indicted Document Forger Evades Police.' And there's a picture of Mason, whose name is actually Gerald Biggs. It says here that Biggs—a.k.a. Mason—worked for a crime ring that specialized in forged documents and false identities."

Polly gasped. "So, the false identity specialist created a false identity for *himself*."

"And his sister." Lulu tapped my screen to scroll down. "Look at this picture. I'm sure this is Dana in the background."

I pinched to zoom on her face. "Different haircut and style of clothing, but yeah. It's her." My heart sank as I pondered the implications. "She duped us all." I set my feelings aside. "The article goes on to say that Gerald—I'll never get used to calling him that—had changed identities more than once. Go figure."

"And then he gave the cops the slip and turned up in Beaver Bluff." Anger laced Polly's voice.

Slowly, everyone went to their own seats, and I passed around the tablet so they could all get a better look. Naomi tilted her head around to see from all angles. "I still don't understand how this helps us figure out who murdered Mason—er, Gerald."

"It doesn't, at least not yet." I drew a deep breath. "But now, we can do more research. What we do know, however, is that he worked with some bad dudes and was wanted by law enforcement."

"We need to tell the police what we know." Lulu re-tied her gray braid.

Verity bit her lip and slightly shook her head. "They won't listen to us unless we come up with proof. Us doing a reverse image search isn't going to make a difference to them, especially since Mason is dead."

"Do you think Dana could be guilty?" Naomi asked.

"Of the murder? No way." I slashed my hand through the air to emphasize the point. "She's devastated. There's no way she could fake that."

Verity's face scrunched with disbelief. "Not necessarily."

"Exactly." Naomi punctuated the air with her finger. "In the mysteries I've read, they always say that someone could feel so bad after murdering a loved one that they appear to be in mourning, when in reality, they're feeling guilty about what they did."

"Obviously, you've taken a liking to Dana, but that doesn't make her innocent." Verity touched my arm.

Defensiveness rose inside me, but I couldn't pinpoint why. "Stop it, you guys. We have to look at all the evidence objectively. So far, none of it points to her."

Polly studied her nails. "Except the fact that she's living here under a fake name."

The group argued back and forth, each person bringing up an old clue or snippet of information. It was like rehashing the crime board all over again, this time with updated intel. There was also more than one mention of Naomi's engagement party that I had to sift out so I could focus on the case.

Suddenly, the ring of my phone cut through the chatter. I swiped to answer. "Hello?"

"Meet me at the gazebo in the town square at ten tonight, and I'll tell you what I know. Come alone," said a woman in a hushed tone. Quickly, she disconnected.

"Who was that?" Lulu frowned.

A brief check of my phone revealed the call came from a number I'd contacted several times. I looked at my friends. "Carla."

Chapter Twenty-Two

CARLA'S DEMAND that I come alone didn't go well with the gang, which was how I found my ear filled with noisy chatter as Pooh Bear and I crossed the town square in the dark. The group phone call we'd started so everyone could listen in turned out not to be my brightest idea.

"It's too cold for a stakeout."

"It's past my bedtime."

"I have to pee."

"Don't worry, KC. I've got your six," Polly added.

I wasn't sure what a six was, but I was glad Polly had it.

We'd arrived downtown early enough to get situated before my clandestine meeting, each of us at different times to not arouse suspicion. Lulu and Naomi huddled together on a park bench. Polly attempted to blend in behind a statue of Beaver Bluff's founder, and Verity sat on the lip of a water fountain that had been turned off for the season.

Meanwhile, I tried to appear casual, just a dog owner out for a late stroll. Naomi tried to make me wear a trench coat, saying everyone wore them in the detective shows she watched, but I'd refused. An investigation was no excuse for poor fashion choices.

A chilly wind whispered through the trees, a lonely backdrop to the clack of Pooh Bear's nails and the tap of my heels against the sidewalk. The empty shops around the square added to the stillness, with only the headlights from an occasional car lighting the square. The scent of wood smoke in the air was a reminder that winter was coming.

"So, are we thinking Carla is the killer now?" Naomi asked.

"Shh," Lulu said right beside her. "We don't know if she's lurking around."

"It could be her, but if not, she must know something. Otherwise, she wouldn't have disappeared," Verity explained. "Then there's the whole skewer in the tire situation. That bumps her to the top of my list."

"But what about that Kai fellow, and the jeweler who told you to stay out of it, and the angry electrician? I can't keep them all straight. I need to see the crime board again."

"Naomi, if you'd been around more, you'd know who our prime suspects are." Polly's terse voice squawked in my ear.

"You're just jealous because I'm spending time with Walter."

"Stop bickering." I adjusted my earbud underneath my hair while simultaneously wrangling Pooh Bear. He preferred jogging at a good clip to meandering through the town square. "All of those people are still under suspicion, mostly because they *all* acted suspiciously."

"And now, with Dana and her false identity, we have more people to consider," Verity said.

"Trust me, it's not her." The look on Dana's face every time I saw her confirmed her innocence, not that it would hold up in a court of law.

"You can't go by your feelings. We can only deal in facts—cold, hard facts," Polly emphasized.

While I knew she was right, my gut refused to believe Dana could be involved. Pooh Bear picked up the pace, and I followed while running through the list of suspects in my head. Based on what I knew for certain—which, admittedly, wasn't much—I wasn't sure how to approach Carla. I'd have to improvise.

Suddenly, the sound of crinkling paper sounded in my ear. "Yikes, what is that?" I reached for my phone and turned down the volume. "Are one of you eating candy?"

"It's Naomi," Lulu confirmed.

"I'm sorry, but stakeouts make me hungry."

"You guys, quiet," Verity whispered frantically. "I think I see her coming."

"Okay, everyone, mute your phones. I can't take the chance of her hearing you." Pooh Bear and I rounded the corner. I adjusted my earbud to make sure it stayed put.

"Roger that," said Polly.

A petite, hooded figure hustled over the dry grass near the gazebo. The person looked both ways and over their shoulder before easing into the shadows near the steps. The faint twinkle lights on the gazebo were no match for the darkness, allowing the figure to stay hidden.

Pooh Bear tugged me along. I glanced at my friends, strategically positioned around the square. At least I wasn't alone. Cautiously, Pooh and I veered from the sidewalk and headed toward the gazebo. Dead grass crunched under my heels, causing Carla to whip her head towards me.

She peeked around the edges of her hood. "Good, you came alone."

I shrugged. "If you're innocent, I can't see why that would matter."

"Of course I'm innocent. I can't take any chances of being seen by anyone. It was risky even meeting you here." Carla leaned against the edge of the gazebo, halfway concealed behind a large bush.

"Hiding from the law is what's risky."

Even the darkness couldn't mask Carla's frown. "What do you think I'm guilty of?"

"Why don't you tell me?" I tugged Pooh Bear closer to my side. "And you can start with slashing my tire." Ire rose inside me that something so awful could happen in broad daylight.

"That's what I came to tell you—it wasn't me." Her words punctured the surrounding silence, then she lowered her voice. "When you sent me that picture, I was horrified you thought it was me."

"Isn't that your skewer?"

"You can get sharp skewers like that in any one of a dozen places."

"Here in Beaver Bluff?" I shook my head. "I doubt it."

"Online, here, whatever. When I picked up my stuff, I was missing more than just the one skewer that was used as a murder weapon." Carla's mouth tightened. "The point is, I didn't do it. But I think I know who did."

"Who?"

"My roommate, Kai."

A chill slithered down my spine. Every road somehow led back to Kai. "How would he get your supplies?"

"Didn't you hear me? We're roommates. Also, sometimes he works for me when I need extra help." Carla hunched into her sweater, and she shot a quick look around the town square. "I think he did it."

"My tire?"

"No...*it*." She bit her lip. "I think he murdered that man."

I leveled my gaze at her. "Isn't that exactly what you'd say if *you* were the killer?"

Carla folded her arms and cast another furtive look around the darkened area. "Don't you remember that day? I know you overheard our conversation when Kai said that man would get what was coming to him. Then *bam*...that night, the dude ends up dead."

I recalled the pictures I'd taken. "And Kai was there. Was he working for you that night at the party?"

"Not really. He helped me bring stuff in, but then he stayed and just blended into the crowd. There was never a freebie he didn't enjoy." A look of disgust crossed her face, which was a far cry from the social media photo that declared them the best roomies ever.

Still, something felt off. I let Pooh Bear's leash out a skosh so he could sniff around. "What was Kai's connection to Mason? What motive could he possibly have to kill him?"

Carla shrugged. "Why does Kai do anything that he does? All I know is that he started freaking out the day after the murder—I mean, more than usual. He started getting all suspicious, and when I confronted him about it, he flipped."

I watched her face for telltale signs of lying, but it was too dark to glean much information from her expression or body language. Still, it seemed like she was shifting blame, though I couldn't pinpoint why. I pulled my coat more tightly around me. "If Kai is guilty, then why are you the one hiding?"

"Because I'm hiding from *him*." Exasperation tinted her tone.

"But I've seen you together." I thought back to the night Polly and I fell asleep in front of her house.

"Not since I had a conversation with him that made me suspicious. After that, I left." She shoved her hands into her pockets. "Look, if you don't believe me, ask the police. They know where to find me."

"They do?"

"There's a murder investigation going on. There's no way I would leave without telling them, especially when one of my utensils was used as the weapon." Carla sighed. "How stupid do you think I am? The police already know everything I just told you."

Apparently, that was the downside of not working with the police. I was a little irritated to realize that for once, I was one step behind them.

Pooh Bear stopped sniffing and crossed back to me, laying his head on my feet. I savored his warmth. "Supposing that everything you're telling me is true, then where's Kai now?" He certainly hadn't been showing up for work.

"I'm not sure. He hung out at the house for a bit, I think. But if I had to guess, I'd say he's staying with his brother." Carla's eyes darted around.

"And his brother is…"

"I don't know his brother. I only met him the one time when he was there, and I was watching TV."

Kai's brother must've been the third shadowy figure in the window. The night Polly and I were there seemed like ages ago, and the memory was vague. But what Carla told me fit with what I'd seen. Was it possible she was telling the truth about everything else?

Carla shivered. "That was the last time I went to my house. I don't want to be there in case Kai comes back. All I can think about is how strange he started acting after the murder." Her jaw clenched. "Can you believe people have even accused me? Sure, it was my skewer, but I had no reason to kill that man. I was nowhere near the kitchen when it happened."

"Can you prove that?" I'd looked at all the pictures myself, and I didn't recall seeing her in any of them close to the time of the murder.

Suddenly, a noise screeched in my ear. I placed my hand over my earbud and hoped Carla didn't hear. Whoever was on the other end needed to mute themselves before Carla got suspicious.

"If I could totally prove it, I'd be off the hook."

"Did the police say you're an official suspect?"

"Isn't everyone who was there?"

No, but I didn't want to tell her that. I let go of my ear, making sure my hair still covered the bud. "Can you tell me anything about Kai's brother, like where I might find him? I think I remember hearing he works for the electrical company too."

"Yeah, they both work there—or did." She cast another look around and rubbed her arms. "That's all I know. I'm going to get out of here. I can't help but feel like he's watching me. I won't feel safe until this whole mess is over."

"Just one more question…why were you upstairs with Kai the day of the murder?"

Carla's eyes narrowed. "He was checking out some wiring, and I tagged along. No biggie."

My earbud squealed, causing me to cringe. "Ouch, stop it."

"What?" Carla asked, wide-eyed.

I shook my head…and my earbud toppled to the ground. Tiny voices telling one another to shut up and mute their phones cried out from somewhere near my shoe. Pooh Bear sniffed the earbud and whimpered at the sound of our friends.

"What's going on?" Carla pushed away from the gazebo and whipped her head around. "Is this a setup?"

"No, of course not." I bent over and scooped the earbud off the ground. "It's just…hey, how can I get in touch with you?"

"You can't." And with that, Carla darted off into the night.

IN RETROSPECT, I should've taken my earbud out before meeting Carla. There'd been no reason for me to have it in. Now we'd scared off the one person who was willing to talk. At least she'd given us snippets of information to help piece together the mystery—if she was telling the truth.

"She could be lying." Lulu pulled a tray of scones out of the oven and set them on the counter.

A hint of peppermint wafted in the air. I resisted the urge to grab one, but only because I knew it would earn me a hand slap. "True, but then why would she have wanted to meet me? Plus, she seemed truly scared. Her body language matched her words." I wadded up my apron and tossed it into the hamper.

Lulu peeled off her oven mitt and palmed my arm. "No offense, but I think your senses are a little off. You're not seeing what the rest of us are, at least when it comes to Dana."

"My senses are not off!" They might've been a little off. Between James still staying in town and having my mind occupied with visions of Hamson and me and a happily ever after, I wasn't on top of my game. We had to be close to an answer, though, or the perp wouldn't have gone to the trouble of messing with my tire.

"Okay, calm down." Lulu glanced toward the swinging door. "Your voice carries. In any case, what's the plan now?"

What, indeed? I leaned against the counter to ponder the afternoon. "I'm going to do a little work here, then head over to the yarn shop to finalize promotions for their fiber event."

"I meant with the case."

"I was getting to that." I reached toward a cooling scone. Lulu whapped my hand, just as I'd suspected she would. "All I can do is keep looking into Dana and Mason's past and see what I can figure out about Kai. Maybe we can try to flush him out of hiding the same way we did Carla."

Lulu wielded her spatula at me. "That sounds like a bad idea. If your mother knew about this, she'd have my head."

"I doubt that." I picked at a hangnail.

"Your parents call me every week to check up on you."

I folded my arms. "Well, they don't call me."

Lulu shot me a searing gaze. "Do you call *them*?"

Touché. I rolled my eyes and headed for the breakroom. "This is not therapy hour. We have work to do." I grabbed my handbag as I mentally tallied my tasks. "Before I start investigating, though, I'm going to get the ball rolling for Naomi's party Friday. Let's see what I can pull together in two days."

Lulu's mouth made a moue of distaste. "Are you sure the B&B is ready for another party so soon after Mason's murder?"

"Dana said it was. She needs the event side of the business to pick up, and having a gathering is a great way to take people's focus off what happened. Besides, who knows what kind of clues we'll pick up about her and Mason's past while we're there?" Lightning fast, I snatched a scone off the tray and took a bite. "Delicious, as usual."

Out front, I grabbed a cinnamon-spiced latte and sat at my favorite table near the window. The soft chatter of customers and music provided the perfect white noise while I worked. I pulled up the party prep checklist template I'd designed after first talking with Dana last week.

A memorable soiree took weeks, if not months, to plan. And I only had days, which meant we'd have to go for the basics. Thankfully, Naomi wanted to keep things small and simple. That meant focusing on decorations, music, and food—not from Carla. Even if I now believed she was innocent, the rest of the gang had their reservations. I worked for twenty minutes or so until I was rudely interrupted.

"Hey, there you are." James whipped out a chair, turned it around, and sat on it backward. "I've been looking for you."

I suppressed a sigh and kept my eyes trained on my tablet. Maybe he'd go away. "What'cha need?"

"Nothing, just wanted to hang out."

"Aren't you still afraid everyone suspects you? It's awfully brave of you to come here." I cast him the briefest glance.

James flashed a winning smile that made people give him second, third, and twentieth chances. "I know I'm innocent, and it's only a matter of time before everyone else realizes that, too. You'll figure it out." He reached out and squeezed my hand. "I have confidence in you."

I jerked my hand back before anyone saw and misunderstood. "If you want me to figure things out, then you'll have to leave me alone so I can work."

"But I'm bored," he whined. "Also, you ran out of shampoo and conditioner."

"What?" I snapped at him. "You used up all my good stuff?"

"We can get more."

"Not in Beaver Bluff." I shut the lid on my tablet. "Seriously, you couldn't have brought your own? If you didn't have so much freakin' hair, I'd still have product left."

James held up his hands. "Chill, babe. I guess I'll order more for you and have it delivered."

"You'd better." I pointed my stylus at him. "Rush. Delivery."

He made a faux-penitent expression. "I guess now's not the time to tell you there's no more coffee at home, either."

I growled.

"I'll just grab some java here." James stood and flipped the chair back around. "Oh, by the way, when I stopped at Polly's to look for you, she said for you to come home. The dogs need a walk."

While James occupied himself chatting up Krystal at the counter, I snuck into the kitchen and said goodbye to Lulu and Bert, who was spraying off some cookware. I sighed with relief when I climbed into my car and sped away without further interaction with James. He wasn't all bad, but the more I talked to him, the more I realized how happy I was in Beaver Bluff. The old life in LA no longer suited me. Everything I wanted was right here, including a certain officer whose heart I planned to win as soon as this whole mess was over.

Minutes later, I rolled into Polly's driveway. Pooh Bear saw me from the window and started his happy bark. A symphony of joyful yips from both my guys greeted me inside. "How are you, little fellas? Did you miss me?" I ruffled their fur, alternating kisses between them.

"I think they're ready to get out and stretch their legs." Polly peered at me over her newspaper from the living room. "They played out back for a while, but my yard's kind of small for them."

"There's time before my appointment this afternoon. I can take them for a short walk." I ruffled their fur again. "Who wants to walk? Who's coming with me?" They both barked, and Pooh Bear trotted over to their toy box and dragged out his leash.

Polly folded her newspaper and set it aside. "So, how are we going to flush Kai out of hiding?"

By now, I shouldn't have been surprised that Polly and I had the same line of thinking. But I was. She was turning out to be a pretty good sidekick. As much as I missed working closely with Verity all the time—and I knew Polly missed Naomi the same way—I was happy that our friends had found love.

I clipped Cujo's leash while I pondered our next move. "I'm not sure. Getting Carla wasn't hard, but Kai is a different story. Carla said he might be with his brother, so maybe our next move is to go back to M&Z Electric and see what we can find." I clipped Pooh's leash. "Oh, maybe we can follow the brother home. That way, we won't even have to talk to the owner."

"Don't we still suspect him too, though?"

"Hmm. Yes and no. He was pretty angry at Mason, but he wasn't at the party."

Polly pushed herself off the couch. "But he still could've snuck in the back door and done the deed."

"True." I sighed. "I guess that's part of the problem—too many leads. We're going to head out." I opened the door. "Be back in a few."

"Hopefully, they'll be ready for a nap when you come home."

I doubted it but didn't want to burst Polly's bubble of hope for a quiet afternoon. Together, my guys and I headed down the sidewalk, enjoying the fresh ocean air rolling in off the bluff. The overcast sky warned of a coming storm. Once it started snowing, these walks would be a little less pleasant, and I'd have to give up my heels. But it *was* a good excuse to buy more cute boots.

The boys and I rounded the corner and headed down the road of the B&B. Maybe I could pop in and talk party plans with Dana and make sure the cleaners had whipped the place into tip-top shape. No one wanted to celebrate pending nuptials near a death spot.

Once again, a white van was parked in front of the B&B. It couldn't be the biohazard cleaners again, could it? We quickened our pace. The sign on the side of the van indicated it was not the biohazard people but M&Z Electric. Again. Hopefully, whatever electrical issues the B&B was having now wouldn't be a problem by Friday night.

"Let's go see what's happening," I said to my pooches. We slowed our approach.

A man wearing a work shirt emerged from the B&B—the same one I'd seen leaving M&Z the other day—and Dana followed him out to the porch. They stood facing each other while talking, then Dana folded her arms, nearly hugging herself. The man reached out and caressed her shoulder, and she didn't pull away. Curious.

I stopped and tugged on the leashes. Pooh Bear looked up at me, as though seeking direction. "Shh." Cujo whimpered but remained still.

The man reached up and swiped the hat off his head, releasing his shaggy hair—hair that I'd seen before but couldn't quite place. Where did I know him from other than M&Z? I watched the pair closely, willing myself to remember.

Dana reached out and palmed the electrician's chest before turning away from him and going back inside. The man secured his hat back on his head and cast his gaze to the ground before descending the steps. He walked around to the driver's side of the van and climbed inside.

And that's when it hit me where I'd seen him before.

I tugged my boys' leashes and hurried them back toward Polly's house. Forget going to the yarn shop to discuss their event. I needed to see Randall the jeweler, pronto.

Chapter Twenty-Four

"YOU, ME—NOW." I pointed from myself to Randall to the back room as soon as the last customer walked out of the jewelry store.

"What on earth?" Randall adjusted his vest in a huff.

Polly shook her head. "She's running on caffeine, pastries, and just a few hours of sleep. If it were me, I'd listen to her." She parked herself on a stool near the diamond case.

Randall lifted his nose with an air of superiority. "I might have customers come in."

"Don't worry. I'll keep watch." Polly glanced around and nodded. "I got this."

I marched behind the counter and headed for Randall's office. His brisk footsteps sounded behind me. "Look, I know you told me to stay out of it, but I can't." I leaned against his desk.

"I have no idea what you're talking about." Randall appeared more curious at this point than angry. "Is this about the winter extravaganza plans?"

Oh, right. I'd forgotten about those. I scratched my head, which was already overloaded with clues, details, and items on my to-do list. "We'll get to that."

"Why are you here demanding to see me?" He sat in his office chair and gestured for me to take the one across from him. "This is highly unusual."

I took a seat and willed my heart rate to slow. Now that I had an audience with Randall, I didn't need to be so worked up. "Sorry, but I need answers, and the last time I was here, you put me off."

Randall looked perplexed. "I'm ready to talk about the extravaganza whenever you are."

"No, not that. Let me start over." I raked my hand through my windblown hair. "I have questions, and I need answers about what happened last Friday night at the B&B."

A wary expression crossed Randall's face, and he rubbed his temple. "You mean Mason's murder."

"Yes."

"I already told you everything I know. I didn't see a thing." He set his elbows on the armrests and folded his hands. "I was just enjoying the night like everyone else."

"I believe you."

"Then why are you here?"

"Because I think you know someone who…knows something." I refused to lay out all my suspicions. Even though my gut told me Randall was basically trustworthy, regardless of his prior warning to me, I wasn't clear on his relationship with the Fulsoms.

"This murder business—it's dangerous." His eyes crinkled at the corners. "Why take chances? Just let the police do their jobs. It'll all sort itself out." The concern in his voice felt genuine.

"Let's just say I have a vested interest in the outcome."

Randall issued an exasperated sigh. "Fine. I don't think I know anything but ask away."

"Tell me about the guy who returned the engagement ring."

"Oh, no, no. I don't do refunds on those. Remember?" He pointed to a printed no-refund policy pinned to the bulletin board above his desk. "I make that very clear to all my customers."

"Ugh. Work with me here." I slapped his desk a few times for effect. "The guy who *wanted* to return the engagement ring."

"Who, Phil?" Randall's forehead wrinkled.

"I guess that's his name." I mulled it over. Where had I heard the name Phil before? "Didn't you say he's a friend of yours?"

"Acquaintance, more like."

"Tomato, to-mah-to." I downplayed the difference, but I was glad to know. That made it less likely Randall would repeat this conversation to Phil. "Just humor me and tell me what you know about your *acquaintance*."

"Nice enough man, I guess." Randall's mouth crimped as he shrugged. "I met him when he was doing some work here. He's an electrician."

"Do you know the woman he proposed to?"

"Nope. Never saw her."

So far, Randall was right—he didn't seem to know anything useful. Still, I pressed on. "I wonder what happened to him after he left? Maybe she changed her mind."

"If not, he may have pawned the ring. Some guys do that when they've been turned down." Randall shook his head. "If you ask me, he dodged a bullet."

"How so?"

"He said she came from a controlling family or something. Married life is hard enough without adding weird relative issues." Randall twirled a pen between his fingers. "Is that all? I need to get back out front. As much as your friend there said she can handle my store, she doesn't actually work here." He smirked and shook his head.

"Yeah, just one more question."

"Shoot." He pointed his pen at me.

"Does Phil have a brother named Kai?"

"I think so." He pushed out of his chair. "Like I said, I don't know him all that well, but that name sounds familiar. It's one of those names that sticks out."

And with that, some pieces fell into place. While I didn't have all the answers, I had a pretty good idea of what happened. Now I had to catch the police up on my intel so they could make an arrest.

"ARE YOU KIDDING? We can't make an arrest based on that." Hamson stared at me like I'd grown a second head.

Other officers in the station peered at us. I should've taken Hamson's offer to talk in an interview room instead of in the group workspace. Slowly, the others returned to their own computers, phones, and reports, though I did catch Officer Leon sneaking another peek at me.

I lowered my voice and hoped Hamson would do the same. "You can't do anything, even after what I just told you? If you think about it, you'll realize my hunch is right."

He eased closer. The fresh scent of shampoo and aftershave wafted off him. "We don't make arrests based on hunches. That's not how this works. Not even close."

"Look, I know you guys have all your official rules and blah blah, but I've figured out who murdered Mason Dunn," I whispered behind my hand. "Which is not his real name, by the way."

"I know that. In fact, we figured that out the first day." The smug look on his face would've been cute at any other time. Instead, it just irritated me.

"Great, I'm glad you're all caught up on that angle. Now, if you'd just listen to the rest of it, we can get this whole mess buttoned up. Like I was telling you, I had this feeling—"

"KC, I believe you have good instincts, but let me make this clear." Hamson rubbed the bridge of his nose. "We work with evidence, facts, there's a chain of command—"

"But all of that takes too long, especially when I've already figured it out. Why waste time?" I scooted my chair a little closer and hooked into his gaze. His eyes, like twin pools of dark chocolate, made it hard to concentrate. "And once this is over, I can send James packing, and then you and I can…"

Hamson's smoldering gaze seared into me, and his mouth curled in a half-smile that stole my breath. "You and I can what?"

I glanced around before speaking. "You know…" I reeled my hand, hoping he'd fill in the blanks.

"I think I have a pretty good idea." Hamson's eyebrow lifted suggestively. He leaned closer and whispered. "Maybe we can think about picking up where we left off."

Officer Leon cleared her throat from a few desks over.

Hamson sat back, then spoke in a police-y tone. "Anyway, thanks for coming in. We'll be in touch if we have further questions." He stood abruptly, clearly expecting me to do the same. He offered a curt nod, effectively dismissing me.

My heart deflated a little as I walked out of the station. The overcast sky matched my mood. If I couldn't get him to listen to me, there was no way those state investigators would, either. Frustration pricked me inside, knowing I'd found the killer, along with their motive, means, and opportunity. My heels tapped a dejected rhythm as I descended the concrete steps.

"KC, wait up," a female voice called behind me.

I turned. "Hi, Officer Leon. I suppose you think my ideas are dumb, too."

Her stoic expression gave nothing away as she caught up to me on the bottom step. I leaned against the handrail and waited to be chastised.

Officer Leon fisted her hands on her slender waist. She looked like a supermodel, despite her police uniform. "I don't recall my partner saying your idea was dumb. Don't put words in his mouth."

I ceded the point. "What did you want to talk to me about?"

She threw a glance over her shoulder. "I'm going to trust you with a little secret, and I expect it to go no further."

I stood a little taller. "Absolutely."

"Word has it that Hamson may be up for a promotion."

"That's amazing. For what?" I grinned. Now it all made sense why Hamson wanted to do everything by the book.

"He put in for the detective spot." Officer Leon raised her brows. "And here's the thing—my partner is the hardest working and most decent person on the force. No one deserves a promotion more than him."

"I would be so happy for him."

She narrowed her eyes and spoke sternly. "I would hate to see anyone or anything mess that up for him."

I pointed to myself. "You mean…"

"That's exactly what I mean. Right now, everyone's got their eyes on him." Officer Leon folded her arms. "Please do *not* drag him into whatever shenanigans you and your crew have going on. Just let the state police do their jobs. Whatever you do, just stay out of it."

"WE CAN'T JUST STAY out of it." Polly pounded her fist on the table.

The gang convened in the breakroom so we could decide what to do. So far, it was a split decision. Polly and Verity wanted to go forward. Lulu and Naomi wanted to follow Officer Leon's advice. Apparently, it was up to me to break the tie.

"After last time, I have no confidence in the police." Verity sipped her coffee. "What if they let them get away?"

I released a whoosh of air, blowing my hair out of my eyes. When this mess was over, I still needed to get a color correction. But the way things were going, it could be a while. I leaned my elbows on the table. "I can see both sides. Right now, there's just no way to set this up."

"Why did Officer Leon come and ask you to stay out of it?" Lulu untied her apron and sat. "That seems unusual for her."

I shrugged, mostly because it was easier than dancing around the truth—that Hamson was up for a promotion. If I was good at anything, it was keeping my word. The sad thought that kept circling back was, what if I was bad for Hamson? While Officer

Leon didn't say that in so many words, the implication stung. I didn't want to ruin his chances.

"We can't let the perp get away with this," Polly pleaded.

"I agree. But what do we do?" I rested my chin on my fist and picked at a scone.

Verity nudged me. "Set a trap, just like the last two times."

My mind spun with ideas. How would we go about laying a trap? I had no personal connection to the killer that would lure them in like before.

But there had to be a way.

We couldn't just allow a murderer to potentially get off the hook. If the state police really were on top of things, they'd already have someone in custody. While I'd tried to go about this the right way and hand all my intel over to the authorities, it hadn't worked out. I practically had a civic duty to get the killer behind bars. As long as I left Hamson out of it, no one could hold him responsible for my shenanigans, as Officer Leon had put it.

"We should just let this go and focus on my engagement party." Naomi blushed. "I can't think of anything else until after my get-together. It's so exciting."

I sat up as thoughts pinged in my head. "Hey, that gives me an idea."

"Oh, no." Lulu flashed me a warning glance. "I don't like the sound of that. And like you said, there's no way to set this up."

"Au contraire." I held up my finger. "We'll use the engagement party to lure them in. We've got to start by getting extra people there. The more witnesses, the less likely the killer will be to get away."

Lulu sighed with resignation. "Here we go again. What do you have in mind?"

"I still need to hash out the details." I poised my finger to my lips. "But I'm going to start with making Carla an offer she can't refuse."

Chapter Twenty-Five

NOTE TO SELF: never plan an engagement party/killer trap at the same time ever again.

With so many particulars to iron out, there was bound to be a wrinkle. By the time Friday evening rolled around, my head was exploding with details ranging from the perfect playlist to satisfy our multi-generational crowd to what to do if the killer didn't show up. (The answer was to continue with the party and then move to Plan B, which we did not yet have.)

But as people started arriving at the B&B, I was fairly confident things would work out.

"How did you get Carla here?" Verity sat with me behind the counter that divided the front room from the dining area. We'd just finished rigging my Bluetooth speaker and were watching Naomi and Walter greet a few friends from bingo.

"I told her that after tonight she could quit looking over her shoulder." Honestly, I hadn't thought it would be that easy, but it was hard for a small business owner to say no to money. The one thing I'd insisted with Carla was no shish kebab.

"I'm glad that at least worked out. Can you imagine if we'd had to cook, too?" Verity adjusted the rhinestone butterfly clip in her updo. "Anyway, we'll have to double our workouts after tonight."

"That's an understatement." The heavenly aroma of barbeque drifted from the chafing dishes. Maybe I could sneak a few extra bites before Griff and Holly arrived. The last thing I needed was my trainer eyeballing me tonight for my food choices.

For throwing the event together at the last minute, it had turned out well. We'd gone with a happily-ever-after fairytale theme—which was, admittedly, incongruent with the buffet selection. The sparkly, Cinderella-type decorations evoked a dreamlike quality, and the glass slipper ice sculpture on a high-top table in the center of the room was sure to be a hit.

James meandered over with a wide grin. He leaned close and whispered in my ear. "I'd love to claim a dance with you before the night's over."

With any luck, it would be his last night in Beaver Bluff. A strange mixture of relief and nostalgia simmered inside me. While James's presence had certainly been unwelcome, it helped me figure some things out, like how much I'd come to love my friends and my new life. If only I could see where Hamson fit into the picture. Would having a relationship with me hold him back in his career? That was the last thing I wanted. Still, life was good, and I trusted it would all work out in the end.

I squeezed James's arm. "Yes, one dance."

He pumped his fist.

"A *short* one…with no touching," I added before he wandered off to check out the buffet table.

Lulu ambled over, along with Polly. My aunt drew a deep breath, as though fortifying her nerves before we set the plan in motion. "How long do you want to wait?"

"I think we should hold off until after we eat. No use in perfectly good food going to waste." I came out from behind the counter. "Let's mingle. It'll look less suspicious."

We called everyone to the dining room and started with a toast. For the next thirty minutes, we ate and talked and moved between guests, helping Naomi be the quintessential hostess. Walter beamed at his bride-to-be and regaled the crowd with the story of how they met. A few guests congregated in the center of the room for some light dancing as the greatest hits of the 1960s played from my speaker on the counter. I was almost sorry we'd have to interrupt the fun with all the murder stuff, but it had to be done.

I scanned the room to see who all had arrived. Along with Naomi and Walter's acquaintances from the senior center, several people who attended the fateful fete last week came, too. Randall and his wife, Griff and Holly, and Benson Michaels were among the guests. Hopefully, people attended for the sake of Naomi and Walter, not just to gawp at what had been the crime scene.

Quietly, I snuck over to Dana, who lingered off to the side of the party. "This all looks great. The pictures I took will look fab on your social media. I'd say it's a successful comeback."

Sorrow tinged her eyes, yet she mustered a smile. "All thanks to you."

I was almost sorry to interrupt the B&B's comeback with the murder stuff, too. But justice had to be served. What better place than where it all started? I used my half-empty champagne flute to point at the small camera mounted on the ceiling. "By the way, is your camera working?"

"Yes, I was checking some footage earlier today." Concern inched across Dana's face. She shifted, and her eyes grew wary. "Why?"

"No reason." I hoped my gentle tone put her at ease. "You just can't be too careful. If you'll excuse me, I'm going to refill my drink." Apprehension crept over me as I second-guessed all our plans. Now that everyone had been through the buffet line, it was the perfect time for the main event.

I strolled toward Polly and whispered in her ear. "Wait another minute or so, then on my go, you can take Dana and Carla into the kitchen. It's important Dana see the fuse box has not been touched, or she won't make the call. Make sure to keep them in the kitchen until you hear us call out."

"Is Lulu ready?" Polly scanned the room.

"I think so. As soon as you walk away with Dana, I'm going to flash the sign." I noted how many people were milling about, and who might be likely to notice what was going on and require damage control.

Most everyone appeared relaxed, enjoying themselves as though this were just another party—including Naomi. The way she breezed through the crowd with Walter at her side made the situation feel natural. I appreciated that she was willing to use her special night to trap the killer and take one for the team. For her sake, I hoped she would remember this party as a good one.

After a few moments, Polly moseyed toward Dana. "Yoo-hoo, can I get your help in the kitchen? You, too, dear." She motioned to Carla.

"Of course. What do you need?" Dana met Polly halfway between them and joined Carla in the dining area.

"It's my stomach. I have certain dietary restrictions, and I was thinking you could…" Her voice faded as the trio walked through the swinging door to the kitchen.

I nodded at Lulu. Verity headed toward me, and we took our positions in the dining area.

Aunt Lulu clapped her hands. "May I have everyone's attention, please?" The guests paused their conversations and dancing to listen. "Let's gather over here with Naomi and Walter as they open their gifts." She motioned to a table we'd set near the front window—away from the dining area.

As the guests wandered to the front of the house, Verity and I shared a look, gave each other a thumbs up, then pulled the plugs…literally. First, we unplugged the food warmers, grateful for the tablecloths that covered our deed. Then, as simultaneously as humanly possible, we cut the power to the lamps near the dining area by rotating the bulbs until the lights cut out. Last, I disconnected the Bluetooth from my speaker, which was plugged into an outlet.

One by one, the guests turned around when the music turned off.

"Oh, no…I think the power went out." Verity enunciated each word as though reading off a teleprompter. Next time—though hopefully there wouldn't *be* a next time—I'd have to give her a role that didn't require even a smidgen of untruth.

"So strange," I said while pretending to check my speaker. "But only in this part of the house."

Murmurs rumbled through the small gathering, likely recounting the similarity to last week's outage. This time, however, the room wasn't cast in total darkness.

"Don't worry. We'll get the music up and running in no time," I assured everyone. "Dana?" I called out.

Dana, Carla, and Polly emerged from the kitchen. Dana frowned. "What's going on?"

I pretended to flick the control on my speaker, then pointed to the lamps and the food warmers. "It looks like the power to this part of the house cut out." I walked closer and spoke in a low tone. "We need good word of mouth for your publicity, which means music and warm food. You need to call your electrician friend right away."

Chapter Twenty-Six

IT DIDN'T TAKE LONG for Dana to check that the switches in the breaker box hadn't flipped. She rushed to call Phil. Meanwhile, the unsuspecting guests hung out with Naomi and Walter while they opened their gifts.

Only James was a problem.

He picked up my speaker, examined it, then quirked his eyebrow. "Care to explain?"

"No." I snatched the speaker back and set it on the counter. "And if you want to have your name cleared, you'll quit asking."

James flashed a devastating grin. "I can't wait to find out what you're up to."

Just then, Phil walked inside the B&B carrying what appeared to be a hefty toolbox. This time, he was dressed in jeans and flannel, rather than his work uniform and hat, looking exactly the way he had the day he tried to return the engagement ring, shaggy hair and all.

He approached the dining area and set his box on the counter while Dana explained what had turned off.

Phil's eyes combed the area, noting which items had gone dark. He pointed to two different lights and the food warmers.

"These aren't even on the same circuit, and the speaker should run on battery."

My heart leaped into my throat. "My batteries are dead—just like Mason," I said loudly enough for the guests to hear.

Phil stiffened as my words hit their target.

Slowly, everyone in the room turned and began to move in our direction.

"That's right. We've figured out what happened last week." I stuttered as people formed a circle around us. Murmurs rose from the crowd.

"I'd like to hear what you're thinking," Benson Michaels said. Others chimed their agreement.

I rubbed the sweat from my hands, not daring to look into Phil's eyes just yet. "At first, we had so many suspects and clues that it was impossible to sort it out." I paced in front of the counter. "There were a number of guests here last Friday who both wanted to murder Mason *and* who had the opportunity when the lights went out. I'm sorry to say, but between the way he leered at me—which I'm sure he did to others—and how much money he owed everyone in town, he was not a popular guy."

Dana sniffled, and Phil clasped her hand for support.

"First, James was an easy target since he'd had a fight with Mason earlier that day." I glanced at him and smiled. "But I knew from personal experience that he didn't have the stomach for it. After he followed Mason into the kitchen, he left up the back stairs."

"Not having the stomach for it—" Benson Michaels used his fingers to air-quote me, "does not clear someone from suspicion."

"It will when you hear the rest." I continued to pace. "If you recall, it was a utensil from Carla's business that killed Mason," I continued.

Everyone in the room gasped as they looked at Carla.

"But it wasn't me!" she protested.

"It wasn't," I agreed. "Then there was one point where I suspected Randall."

Everyone turned to look at the vested jeweler. He palmed his chest. "Me? How dare you."

"Come on, after the way you warned me not to investigate? It totally made you look suspicious." I gestured for emphasis. "But I remembered that I'd overheard a person saying Mason would get what he deserved, someone who apparently had a bone to pick with Mason. After reviewing video footage, we began to suspect Carla's partner in crime, Kai. Even Carla suspected him."

Carla's eyes rounded, and she shook her head as if to warn me to stop speaking.

"At this point, all roads led to Kai…but only because he was covering up for someone else." I glanced around, wishing he'd been there. But his presence wasn't necessary.

"Covering up?" Carla's eyebrows shot up. "Is that why he's been in hiding, not because he's guilty?"

"Exactly," I said. "I'm guessing that's also why he ran from me."

"What are you getting at?" Dana demanded. Her pitch rose. "Can you just tell us who did it?"

"The murderer was someone who had knowledge of the electrical issues here, *and* someone who knew where to sneak in, *and* someone who was here the day my tire was slashed." I turned and pointed. "And that person is Kai's brother, who wanted to marry Dana." I pointed toward Dana and the electrician. "It was Phil!"

He dropped Dana's hand and shouted. "You have no proof of that!"

"Don't I?" Actually, I didn't. What I needed was to goad him into a confession that would be caught on camera. Even if it couldn't be used for a conviction, it would lend enough credence to point the police in the right direction along with multiple witnesses who would testify.

Chatter rippled through the crowd as each person tried to ascertain whether or not I was correct. Everyone shifted uneasily. I heard the door open and close, but I didn't dare turn to look. As long as we contained Phil, that was all that mattered.

I looked at the electrician. "You wanted to be with Dana and thought that if Mason was out of the way, you could get married."

Dana covered her mouth. "How would you know any of this?"

"I made the connection after seeing Phil here with you on the porch, and then I talked to Randall. And once I realized you and Mason had a past, I knew why he wanted to prevent you from getting married." I stopped short of revealing Dana's history. Some things would be up to her to sort out later. I softened my voice as I spoke to her. "I remember you said you came here for a fresh start and that you were almost happy."

"I was," she said with sorrow.

"Randall told me you wouldn't marry Phil because of your controlling brother. Mason was going to make you move again, wasn't he? That was part of his hesitation when I first wanted to help you guys build this business. But he needed to keep running." I offered Dana a sad smile. "You were a loyal sister to stick with him through everything."

Dana buried her face in her hands as she nodded. Then she spoke through her tears. "Is it true, Phil?" She dared to look at him. "It is, isn't it? I hoped I was wrong, but I suspected all along." Her voice hitched.

"Is that why you denied knowing Kai when I showed you the video?" I asked.

She offered a faint nod. "The video wasn't proof, so I wanted to keep quiet."

"But Mason was your brother," I argued.

"And we had a complicated relationship." Her firm tone differed from the demure Dana I'd come to know. "And I didn't want anything that led back to Phil."

"I didn't do anything." Phil's jaw clenched. "It's all bull."

"Why did you suspect him?" I ignored Phil and hoped Dana would fill in some missing pieces.

"I saw him in the kitchen not long before the lights went out that night. I told him to wait for me and that I'd talk to him after the party."

I remembered the nook in the back room where he'd have stayed out of sight. Where neither James nor Mason could see him. When James went up the back stairs, it was the perfect opportunity for Phil to take out Mason.

Dana turned to face Phil. "But when everything was over, you were gone. I didn't want to believe it, but it's true."

Redness crept up Phil's neck and settled in his face, and his lips turned white. "All I wanted was to be with you, and this is where it got me!" He stalked away from the dining area and pushed through the crowd.

"Stop him!" I shouted as I followed. But rather than guests circling around him, they parted like the Red Sea to let him pass.

Until he ran into Hamson.

My breath caught in my throat as I drank in the sight of Hamson, who stood in front of the door, arms folded across the expanse of his chest. "Not so fast."

Phil turned and bolted back toward the dining room. He grabbed the lip of the table in the center of the room and shoved it back towards Hamson. The ice sculpture flew through the air and landed on the floor, shattering. But it only stopped Hamson for a moment.

Anger flashed in Phil's eyes as he barreled toward the kitchen. I stepped into his path. Then, I pivoted and kicked out with my foot, aiming for his kneecap. Pain exploded up my leg on contact.

Phil's arms pinwheeled. He flew backward and slammed into the fallen table. His body hit the floor with a thud. The crowd sent up a collective gasp, then closed in around him. Hamson stood over Phil with a look that dared the perp to try to escape again.

I clutched my chest as adrenaline shot through my veins. Hamson glanced over at me, his expression unreadable. Though I couldn't begin to guess what was going through his mind, one thing was sure—he'd been there for me when it counted.

James appeared at my side and clapped my back. "Dude, that was sick."

"Dude," I said, matching his tone. "You have no idea."

Chapter Twenty-Seven

THE WEATHER TURNED OVERNIGHT, kicking fall out the door and ushering in winter. The day after Naomi's engagement soiree, snow fell lazily from the sky, changing our post-murder wrap-up barbecue into an indoor pizza party. The gang—plus Walter, David, and James—crowded into my tiny living room.

"Honestly? I didn't think the plan would work. There's so much that could've gone wrong." Aunt Lulu bit into a slice of deep-dish pepperoni.

"Nonsense." Polly waved her off. "KC and I had it under control the whole time."

"Well, I don't know about the *whole* time. But we're pretty good at thinking on our feet, so we would've come up with something." I shared a corner of my garlic knot with Pooh Bear. "I think we did pretty well, considering we're amateurs. It's not like there's a book on how to solve crimes."

Verity cleared her throat. "Uh, there are literally hundreds of books on how to do this stuff."

Everyone groaned. Then Walter laughed and slapped his knee. "The only thing that matters to me is that my bride-to-be looked beautiful and had a good time. I can't wait to make her my wife." He slung his arm around Naomi and squeezed.

"Oh, Walter. I love it when you talk like that." She giggled like a teenager in love.

David, with his dark hair and brooding eyes, cuddled with Verity on the couch. They wore the same contented expressions on their faces as the older couple. Polly and I shared a look and sighed. Including the men in our group would take some getting used to, especially considering not all of us were so lucky in love. My thoughts wandered back to Hamson, as they had so many times over the last twenty-four hours.

"Have you two settled on a date?" Polly set down her empty plate.

Naomi's cheeks bunched when she smiled. "We're going to have a Christmas wedding!"

Lulu sat tall. "*This* Christmas?"

Naomi and Walter both nodded with excitement. Cheers went up in the room, along with a hearty round of congratulations. It looked like our cozy group was changing for good. And from the looks of it, Verity and David wouldn't be far behind. Both joy and wistfulness swelled in my heart as I looked ahead to the planning and preparations.

I grabbed the empty pizza box off the coffee table and headed for the kitchen. James followed, and the pups came behind him. "Did you get everything packed up?" I asked.

"Yeah." A smidgen of longing crept into his voice. "I guess it's time for me to head out, but I wanted to thank you."

"For what?" I rinsed the plates in the sink.

"Everything." He cupped my shoulders and turned me to face him. "For believing in me when no one else did."

I leaned into a quick hug. "At least let me know you made it back home safely." I glanced out the patio door at the fluffy flakes falling from the sky. It seemed a nice way to close this chapter of my life.

James made the rounds, telling each of my friends goodbye. He even stopped to pet my pups before slipping on his shoes. Then he grabbed his messenger bag and rolling suitcase.

I tugged open the door. Hamson stood on the porch, his hand poised to knock. My pulse skipped at the sight of him, snowflakes on his dark hair and hope in his eyes. "You're here." A gust of snowy air blew inside.

Hamson burrowed into his thick flannel coat. "I heard there was a gathering."

"Oh, brother." James offered a good-natured laugh, then reached out for a fist bump from Hamson. "Take care of this one." He cocked his head toward me. "She's a firecracker, and she'll keep you on your toes, but she's worth every minute. It's too bad I learned that too late." And with that, he tightened his man bun and walked out the door.

"Come in." I grabbed Hamson's coat and pulled him inside, where the gang offered up rounds of hellos. The dogs greeted him with indifferent sniffs until he pulled treats out of his pocket and tossed them in the air for them to catch.

As Pooh Bear and Cujo settled down, my friends and their boyfriends got up and made excuses for hitting the road. A flurry of coats and hats and leftovers ensued, along with promises to get in touch tomorrow.

"I hope they're not leaving because of me," Hamson whispered in my ear, sending a tingle down my spine.

"They're leaving precisely because of you." My face grew warm as my friends filed out the front door. Nothing like being obvious. I shoved the door closed and turned to Hamson. "You'll have to forgive them. They need a little work on their subterfuge skills."

"Oh, I don't know about that. I hear things went pretty smoothly before I got there last night—subterfuge skills and all." Hamson sat on the arm of the couch and ruffled Pooh's ears.

I scooped Cujo up to pet him and hide my nerves. Standing this close to Antonio Hamson sent my heart into a tailspin. "How did you even know about the event last night?"

Hamson scoffed. "When KC Crumb throws a party, people talk. I'm pretty sure the whole town knew about it." He smiled at me, his dimples deepening. "And knowing you, there would be more to the party than food and music."

"I'm that predictable, huh?"

"Predictably unpredictable, more like it." His finger trailed down my arm, then rested on Cujo.

Thoughts of Officer Leon's warning pinged in my head. While I wanted to go forward with whatever was happening between Hamson and me, I wanted what was best for him. It was better to know now than later. I drew a shaky breath. "Dare I ask if you got in trouble for showing up?"

"I was there unofficially, so no."

Relief swirled inside me. "Your partner had a talk with me." I searched Hamson's eyes. "I was worried that having anything to do with me would be a problem."

Hamson reached out and squeezed my hand gently before letting go. "You let me worry about Officer Leon and the others. I'll be fine."

I tried to tame my smile and lost. But before we went too far, I wanted more answers about last night. "What ended up happening to Phil?"

"You saw him get arrested for disorderly conduct, right?"

I thought back to the officers on patrol arriving and hauling Phil away in handcuffs—and the distraught look on Dana's face when it happened. Pandemonium followed until we settled the crowd and finally wrapped up the party.

"Well," Hamson continued, "after a few hours in an interview room, he broke down and confessed to the murder and to slashing your tire, too. Of course, nothing's going to happen with the murder investigation unless the evidence comes back and confirms it. Looks like the state police and the lab have their work cut out for them."

"And what about Dana?"

"I'll be honest. She's got some problems heading her way. When she came in for questioning this morning, her brother's whole identity theft connection came out, and of course she'd known about Phil being at the B&B the night of the murder and never said anything. She wasn't directly involved in either situation, but she was an accessory after the fact. The DA is going to have a lot to sort through." Hamson blew out a long, minty breath and shook his head. "In the end, the truth will come out."

I ventured closer to Hamson, my leg brushing his knee. "I'm glad all that's over with. At least as far as we're concerned."

"We? I like the sound of that." Hamson's eyebrows tented suggestively as he met my gaze. He cupped my elbow and drew me closer to his position on the couch's arm. Then he took Cujo from me and set him down before grasping my hand. "So…you actually sent James packing."

"Just like I said I would." I straightened Hamson's collar. "There's only one man I'm interested in."

Hamson seared me with a dark, smoldering gaze. "Do tell."

"This certain man seems to enjoy playing hard to get." I tapped his chest.

Hamson tilted his head and gazed up at me. "Is that so?"

"Yeah, but I'm sure he'll make it worth the wait." I allowed Hamson to reel me toward him. "What about you? Is there someone you're interested in?"

"Indeed, there is." Hamson's eyebrows quirked. "But she seems to have a thing for man buns."

"Oh, trust me—she's over that phase." Way over.

"In any case, I've been told she's a firecracker, but I like her that way. I hope I get a shot with her." Hamson rose slowly until he stood over me and his breath whispered over my face.

I swallowed, willing myself to stay calm as I inched ever closer. "What would you do…*if* you were lucky enough to get a shot?"

Hamson leaned down until his lips brushed mine, first gently and then with a quiet urgency. He held me tightly against his rock-solid chest and stroked my hair. Then he pulled back and spoke, his voice full of conviction. "I'd never let her go."

I melted into Hamson's embrace. My heart soared at the thought of what the future might hold for Hamson and me. Life had, indeed, taken a turn for the better. Now that we had the investigation behind us, there was nothing to keep us apart. After all, what were the odds of another murder happening in Beaver Bluff?

THE END

THANK you for following along with the adventures of KC and her gang! If you enjoyed the book, please remember to leave a review.

Join my newsletter and receive *The Mystery of the Missing Groom,* a Beaver Bluff Short Mystery featuring our pal Verity, for free!

Stay tuned for more fun with book 4, *Crumbs of Christmas Past.* Until then, love and crumbs!

Acknowledgments

The usual suspects were involved in creating this book. Without them, *Crumbs* would be nothing but a pile of words!

George and Tessie Moate, Troy Daniels, Mallory Cornelius, Chloe Daniels, Tori Daniels, Betsy Haddox, Dineen Miller, Kristin Avila, and Liz Winney—thank you for all the love, support, help, grace, and generosity! If only every writer had a team like mine. I'm truly blessed!

Special thanks to Team Crumbs for helping me spread the word. Each of you bring a smile to my face!